Nicholas E

Oligarch

Oligarch

Also by Nicholas E Watkins

Tanker

Dealer

Bank

Steel

Hack

Nicholas E Watkins

About the Author

Nicholas Watkins lives on the Coast with his wife and has four children

He is a retired Accountant and has a Degree in Economics. He worked in

the City of London for many years.

Oligarch

Chapter 1

Aleena heard the news that her husband had been killed in the fighting in Mosul, Iraq, not with a sense of grief, but with fear. She was fourteen years of age and had travelled with her sister and her friend to Iraq, just four months ago. They had been seduced by the ISIS propaganda on the internet, with heads filled with dreams of playing their part in the restoration of the Caliphate and a perfect World in which they fitted, they had left Walsall and headed for Iraq. They were to be brides to the brave fighters in a Holy War.

Their dreams soon evaporated like early morning mist, as the reality of the situation was revealed. Her sister and friend, Mariam and Haniya, had become the camp whores. They had no choice. The Jihadis used any unmarried women that way. To justify their actions, they would brand young girls as unclean. Unclean could mean anything from using tampons, to shaving their pubic hair. Anything would do in order to justify the mass raping of young women in the local population, or so called Jihadi brides from abroad. It made no difference. All in the name of Allah and always justified by some obscure and misinterpreted verse in the Qur'an

She had been more fortunate in that she had not been raped to death in the preceding months. She had been taken by an ISIS lieutenant as his bride. Her being more fortunate was relative. He was old with rotting teeth, rotting body and a rotting soul. He had used her as he wished, enjoying the privilege he had to take and keep a young girl for himself to the full. She had never felt so much pain as he had inflicted on her young body. She now constantly bled from her anus, which was completely prolapsed, from his brutal attention.

She was glad he was dead, but she knew that she would be just another whore in the camp, to be gang raped by all the heroes of the Jihad. She huddled in fear as night approached. She had crawled through an opening in the wall to one of the partially collapsed buildings in the compound. She could hear the sounds of shelling in the distance, as she burrowed into the loose rubble in an attempt to conceal herself.

ISIS was losing ground on all fronts. In Syria, Assad's forces, supported by the Russian air force, were driving them out. In Iraq, they were being driven from the territory they held by the Iraqis and the Kurdish forces and the battle for Mosul was almost lost. Morale was low and discipline was breaking down. The fanaticism remained, but was insufficient on its own to win a war.

"Where are you, British slut?" she could hear them getting closer, looking for their evenings entertainment. They called, mocking as you would call your dog. "Here whore, come slut, come, fucky-fucky time."

She tried to hide in the dust and filth of the rubble. She closed her eyes, as if that would have the effect of making her invisible. As if, not seeing the beam of their torches searching the bomb site of what had been a village, would make them not see her. "There you are bitch." Roughly, she was dragged from the building into the compound, where the camp fire burned.

Three women were already being used by the group of, thirty something odd, men. "Another whore to fuck boys," shouted her captures, as she was dragged into the light. Her clothing was ripped from her as she was thrust into the centre to join the gang rape in progress.

She was pushed face down into the dirt, her bottom exposed to the group of men leering at her young, not fully formed body. "Look at her arse hole," said one.

"Fuck me, what a fucking mess. That's been well fisted and fucked."

"Looks fucking nice to me" said another, as he shoved her face further into the dirt and shoved his hard penis, fully in. She screamed in pain as he pushed her prolapsed anus back into her body. The pain was terrible as he thrust with no form of lubrication.

"Fuck, that feels good," he cried as he ejaculated. The queue formed as they waited their turns.

Nizar had had a shit day. He was supposed to be in command. The idea of command was rapidly descending into the theoretical. The Iraqi troops were squeezing them in the South and the Peshmerga were linking up in a pincer move so, the ISIS forces would soon be split in two, The Peshmerga were the troops of the autonomous Kurdish region of Iraq. He knew they were lost. The allies, led by the US, the Russians and local Syrian and Iraqi forces, would regain the ground ISIS had held up until now. It was only a matter of time.

He sat in the Jeep, on his own, looking at the flashes of light over Mosul. The bombardment was incessant now. He had enough of this fucking shit. He had been fighting for four years non-stop. He was losing faith in the dream. It had seemed so different, in what was a lifetime ago, at University in Leeds. Then, he had believed. The lure of a pure Islamic state had seemed so beguiling. In England, he had been disgusted by the society with its secularism and its corrupting influence on his brothers and sister. A land run, in accordance with Sharia law, was what his fellow students and he, who attended the Mosque, wanted. Not the corrupt secularism, in which they lived.

Now he was older and battle weary. The atrocities he had witnessed by ISIS on fellow Muslims, in the name of Allah, had started the worm of doubt burrowing in his mind. He had doubted his faith, which was once so all pervading. He had begun to doubt his own humanity. He was the leader in this sector and he had participated in the beheadings, the rape and the torture. It was all so black and white, when he had begun. If you didn't agree with the ISIS doctrine, you were an enemy and that justified everything.

Nizar no longer believed and he wanted to go home. He started the engine and drove towards the compound.

Aleena was screaming and praying for death as yet another Jihadi began to bugger her. She did not hear Nizar's jeep drive into the compound. The raping soldiers of ISIS paid little heed either as their leader drove up. He stepped from the jeep and looked at the scene with disgust. So this was what he was fighting for. This was the dream he had seen in his minds eye in the Mosque, listening to the Imam's preaching in England. The reality, he now knew, was a crock of shit.

He looked at the girl being gang raped, no more than fifteen or sixteen. Something snapped. He had come to issue the orders and outline this unit's plan of action for the next day. Now, he just wanted them to fuck off.

He snapped. He unleashed a burst of gunfire into the night sky. He had their attention. "Stop fucking and listen to me." They formed a circle around him. He gave the usual bullshit, morale-boosting talk and outlined their role in the next days fight.

They listened, but were eager to return to their evening's entertainment. Their time was running out. They would fight and continue to fight, but they would soon die. The force against them was now overwhelming and it was only a matter of time. There might be virgins in paradise awaiting them, but there was pussy closer to hand now.

He finished his speech, then said, "I'll take the girl."

They were reluctant, but defying their commander was not an option. She gathered her clothes and made her way to the jeep. "Get in."

She sat like a bundle of rags in the back, as he drove away from the compound. She looked at him fearful, expecting them to stop at any moment. What was his particular perversion that made him reluctant to use her in front of the crowd?

"We're going home," he said to her surprise, as they drove west.

Chapter 2

It was early December and the morning was cold, wet and grey. The press were gathered outside East Finchley Crematorium. They sensed there was a bigger story out there, but they just couldn't sniff it out. A Mother and her son were to be cremated today. A Mother who had shot her own son and then had turned the gun on herself was a big story. But, when that Mother had also been the Head of MI5, then it was a truly big story.

They knew there had to be more. They wanted to know what was going on at MI5. Only two months previously, the Deputy Head had been shot in Crete along with the wife of the now acting head, Anthony Burr. They knew that something was going badly wrong in the Service, but they could not ferret out the details.

The inquest into the death of Nicholas Wilkins, at the hands of his Mother Elaine, ruled unlawful killing. No motive was established and vague evidence was introduced, questioning her mental state. Although it made no sense, that the head of MI5 seemed to have left her office, drove to her son's house and shot him. That was what had, apparently, happened. There was no evidence of any third party involvement. She shot him and shot herself. Questions were asked in the House, but not answered. National security was paramount and revealing details of Elaine Wilkins's current operational involvements would not be in the best interest of the Country. That was the line and it was being held to.

The death of Jeff Stiles, the then Deputy Head of MI5 and Jackie

Burr, the wife of the now acting head, Anthony, was just as obscure. There were many unanswered questions, surrounding their murders, but few answers. Mr and Mrs Burr had finished they honeymoon and had meet up with their colleague in Crete, before returning to the UK. Both had been shot, execution style, but the Greek police had made no progress in tracking down the killer.

The one man, who knew all the answers, was Anthony Burr, now head, at least for the moment, of MI5, but he had no intention of filling in the blanks. He was known as Tim. It was a schoolboy nickname that he had found hard to shake off.

Tim Burr stepped from his MI5 issue Jaguar XF and followed, by the driver, who had previously served Elaine, walked passed the press to the Crematorium. The building was modern and red brick. Owing to the drizzle, many of the mourners were gathered under the portico, which afforded some shelter from the drizzle. Tim stood alone, waiting for the hearse to arrive.

This last year had been the stuff of nightmares. He had nearly been killed by terrorists and hunted by the Turkish Secret Service. He had met and married a beautiful woman, had her snatched from him and murdered with his best friend Jeff Stiles. He had found his wife's killer and seen justice done. Her killer had pulled the trigger, but Tim knew that the reason that bullet had been fired, was that men more powerful than the killer, greedy men, had set in motion a chain of events that led, ultimately, to her slaying.

Tim had unfinished business with these men. They had not ordered his wife's murder, nor had they pulled the trigger, but their ambition, greed and thirst for power, had led to the murder. They were her true assassins. For now, they were untouchable, but Tim knew his time would come. Now, as acting head of MI5, he had the resources to hurt these men. He determined that he would bend all to their destruction and they would pay. No matter how long it took, or where they went, he would exact retribution.

Both the Foreign Secretary and the Home Secretary were among the mourners. They arrived separately. Tim knew them both and they acknowledged him. The head of MI6 appeared. All had their security in tow. As more great and good arrived, the number of Special Branch officers assigned to personal protection began to swell, until they formed a small security army. Not only were the Special Branch represented en-mass at the funeral, but the police were highly visible around the Crematorium and spread throughout the local area. There was a massive MI5 undercover presence in Tim's honour, but also to protect the thirty, or so, of his staff from Thames House, who had known and worked for Elaine.

The Prime Minister could not attend. Her duties overseas had prevented her, but the Foreign secretary, Terrance Mailer, who had been with her, had flown back to attend. Tim and Mailer had history. Mailer had been indiscrete in the past and Tim held the evidence that could see him and prison and wreck his life. Tim had used this evidence before to his advantage and he knew that he would again in the future. Tim held Mailer in contempt and knew that he should, rightly, be imprisoned, but that did not matter for now. That could wait. For now, he would do what he had to do to settle the score with the men who had been responsible for his wife's death.

He understood that he was a compromise as head of MI5. He had neither the experience, nor the expertise, for the job. What he had, was the fact that he was alive. He also, had the support of Mailer, purely for his own self-preservation. Tim, however, was good at the job, even if his underlying driving force was revenge. In fact, that revenge gave him an intensity that the service had been lacking under Elaine Wilkins.

The hearse arrived, driving slowly up the sweeping drive, past the garden of remembrance to the side of the building. Elaine's cremation was not the first, nor would it be the last of the day and the flowers in the garden bore witness to that fact. The arrival of the hearse, signalled to the mourners of the previous ceremony, that it was time for their departure.

They followed the coffin in. Elaine's husband followed the pallbearers, pushed in his wheel chair by his brother. Tim followed the two senior Government Ministers, who in the turn followed her immediate family. Her son, Nicholas, was already laid to rest at her local Church. So they were spared the double service. The fact that Elaine's husband had only a few days ago buried his son was apparent in his whole demeanour. He was bewildered and uncomprehending of the tragedy that had occurred. He had not expected to outlive them, but fate had left him alone, to bury his wife and his only son. He had been told that he had only weeks to live five months ago. Fate had been unkind to him, by allowing him to survive long enough to put him through this.

The service was simple and the eulogy was delivered by the priest. Her husband, even if he had wished to say something, could no longer speak clearly, as the paralysis crept incessantly onward through his body.

The curtain opened and the coffin rolled from view to the waiting flames. They trooped out through the side entrance and gathered awkwardly, in silence, into the garden of remembrance. The rain was falling harder as they stood waiting for a respectful interval to pass so they could make their departure without unseemly haste. There was to be a gathering after, but for the Government Officials to attend, they would have filled the venue with so many security personnel as to make it impractical and turn it into a circus. In any event, the presence of so many reporters was already disruptive and no one wanted to add to the situation.

Tim was about to leave when Elaine's husband beckoned to him. He made his way over to the frail man seated in the wheelchair. Tim shook his hand and offered his sympathies. He struggled to understand his speech. His condition had worsened to such an extent that even talking was a challenge. Tim looked to her

13

husband's brother, for clarification.

"Come to the house."

"I shall certainly try, I will find some time and organise it." Tim had no real desire to visit and was making the appropriate response expected of people in these circumstances.

Tim saw this as an opportune moment to restate his commiserations and depart. The man in the wheelchair however, became agitated at Tim's obvious lip service to convention.

His bother took Tim's arm firmly." He insists that you come to the house. It is important apparently. He says Elaine had something there."

"What is it? "

Tim struggled to understand what her husband said in reply. He looked to the man's brother for clarification. "He does not know. He has allowed no one to touch it. It is marked secret."

He looked down at the dying man in the wheel chair and spoke. "I shall come tomorrow. Again I am so sorry for your loss."

Chapter 3

Rafiq wandered down Afghanistan Street to the Three Idiots Restaurant. The rumours were running thick and fast through the Camp. It was inevitable that the Calais and French authorities would have to act to clear the migrant camp, known as the Jungle. Its population was getting close to the ten thousand mark now and was almost a small town with shops, restaurants, nightclubs and even hairdressers. The inhabitants had congregated on this patch of land on the French coast with the common goal of, somehow, getting across the Channel and into the UK.

The Jungle was to be cleared and the French Police, with bulldozers, were assembling. Busses had been arranged to distribute the refugees throughout France and register them. Many, in the Camp, had had enough of living in tents, shipping containers and roughly constructed huts made from scrap. They were leaving for the busses and would start their new lives in France. Others were not so accepting and would not give up their efforts to get cross the Channel. It was this group that Rafiq was interested in.

Sitting in the plastic chair outside the restaurant eating his meal of chicken and rice, he observed the hustle and bustle of camp life. There were plans to start fires and destroy the camp before the Authorities took full control.

"What is happening my man?" Rafiq called to a fellow Afghan, who approached the restaurant.

The young man joined him, with his meal costing about three

euros. "We are not going quietly. We intend to torch the camp tonight. Are you with us?"

With a full mouth, he nodded. Rafiq knew it was important to stay at the centre of things. Hidden among the genuine migrants, he knew were groups whose purpose was not to seek asylum, but to wreck terror and death on the UK. The summer onslaught on the European Borders, by thousands of refugees fleeing the conflicts, across the Middle East had given these terrorist an unprecedented opportunity to get their people into Europe.

"Some of us are planning to move further along the coast and start a new camp."

"Count me in," said Rafiq.

Rafiq, had over the last three months, made sure his credentials, as a man with extreme views, had been spread around the inhabitants of the Jungle. His hard line views had made many wary of him and they made a point of avoiding any association with him. Others had been drawn to his fundamentalist beliefs. They were the people that he and MI5 were interested in.

He was part of the recruitment drive, undertaken by the Secret Service, to ensure they could effectively monitor the Islamic community in the UK. Prior to 9/11. MI5 had historically been focussed on home-grown terrorists such as the Irish. They had been ill equipped to deal with the threat from the Middle Eastern groups. Predominantly white and with no links to the Muslims in the Country, they were disadvantaged in their counter intelligence role. It had to change.

Efforts were made with varying degrees of success. Rafiq, not his real name, was part of the drive, to recruit agents who would blend into the Asian and Muslim community. Following the terrorist attacks in France, in which some of the perpetrators had gained access to the Country posing as refugees. It became imperative that the Jungle needed to be infiltrated. MI5 had taken the lead, as it was considered a counter espionage operation, rather than MI6, who themselves were playing catch-up with Russia, now again added to its list of potential enemies. Along with China, the Middle East and North Korea, MI6 were running to stand still.

Rafiq found himself moved from a comfy flat share in Leicester, to a wet muddy tent outside Calais. Life as an MI5 agent was far less glamorous than he thought it would be when he applied for the job after leaving University. He had been born in the UK. His parents had been in the UK when the Taliban took control in their homeland. They had just not bothered to go back and were granted asylum. They had started a small business and had been reasonably successful. His Mother had not really bothered to learn English and he had consequently grown up bilingual. Only having conversed with his Mother, he developed her regional accent and local vagaries of speech, which made him sound genuinely Afghani.

Over the past months, he had been successful in identifying potential suspects and passed details back to Thames House, the headquarters of MI5 in London. These details had been shared with France and the other EU Countries so their activities could be monitored. The French and others, of course, had their agents circulating in the Jungle as well and he had popped up on their lists as a potential threat. Their agents, had in turn, been added to his list. The various countries secret services would, eventually, sort it between them.

He had spotted the young couple a week ago. They stood out to him. They seemed like genuine refugees at first glance. Rafiq had made it his business to get on the impromptu welcome and orientation committee for new arrivals. This gave him a good opportunity to vet the new arrivals first hand.

The man was in his late twenties and the girl was younger, under eighteen he guessed. They were posing as man and wife. Rafiq felt that there was something amiss. He had developed a feel for the normal inhabitants. These stood out. Firstly, the majority of the arrivals were young men on their own, or in groups. A young couple was far rarer. There was also something about the male that grabbed Rafiq's attention, something about his demeanour that set him apart. It took awhile for him to put his finger on it, but eventually, it became clear in his mind. He was a battle-hardened soldier, not a traumatised civilian fleeing Syria, Iraq or other area of conflict. Something set him apart, confidence, the way he moved, Rafiq was not sure of the indicator, but something set off the alarm in his head.

He made a point of getting close to the couple. Immediately the man spoke, he had his confirmation. The accent gave it away. He was British. The girl also gave their origin away when she spoke, which she tried to avoid doing as much as possible. Rafiq was pretty sure she was a Brummy, or had lived somewhere close to Birmingham.

He knew that the two were, most likely, returning terrorists trying to get back to the UK and avoid being arrested. He was right; Nizar and Aleena had made their way back from Mosul and wanted to get home. They were stuck in Calais however.

That night, fire began to ravage the tents and huts in the Jungle. They had to leave. They couldn't join the queues for the busses that would settle them in France. They could not risk registration. Any inquiry would expose Nizar as a high placed officer in ISIS. As the flames and smoke rose into the night sky, over the camp, he and Aleena gathered together the meagre possessions and made to leave.

They headed north along the coast, avoiding the French Police ringing the camp, under the cover of darkness and the confusion wrecked by the inferno, now raging. Nizar had no plan, but knew the Jungle now afforded no protection for them. Aleena clung to him, still fearful and totally dependant on him. He pulled her close. She had suffered so much and he had given so much for something that neither of them now believed in.

Rafiq followed them as they walked off into the cold and lonely night.

Chapter 4

Tim sat at his desk in Thames House, the headquarters of MI5. Harriet Shaw knocked on the door, "Alright to come in?"

Harriet had been part of the recent recruitment drive to bring in more cyber expertise. MI5 had realised that the new cold war being raged was in cyberspace and like the rise in Middle East terrorism; they were playing catch-up in counter espionage. They were gradually getting their act in order and she had been part of the first crop of recruits. Tim used her as his go to person on internet matters.

"Just sit there for a minute while I finish reading this file."

The trip to Elaine Wilkins's house had been undertaken with some reluctance on his part. Whilst he did have some sympathy for her husband losing both his wife and son at his wife's hand, it only extended so far. His wife and her son had, in the final analysis, been responsible for the murder of his wife

John Wilkins was sat in his wheel chair as the nurse opened the door and showed Tim into the front room. He seemed pleased to see Tim as he sat down on the sofa opposite him. Communication was difficult as his speech was getting worse daily. Tim's hearing gradually tuned into the slurred indistinct voice coming from the man's mouth.

"How are you?" The nurse brought a cup of tea for Tim. Elaine's husband's tea came in a sealed container, like that used as a trainer cup for babies. She held the cup to his lips allowing him to sip through the mouthpiece in the lid.

"I am ok, just feeling a bit sorry for myself."

"I am sorry for your loss. I know you have questions, but I am afraid I really can't add to what you have already been told. Even if I knew more, I wouldn't be able to expand on the details surrounding your wife and son's death." Tim lied.

"I know." His eyes lowered and the pain was clearly evident in his face. It was also clear that he was struggling to understand how his wife had ended up shooting her own son and then killing herself. How could Tim say to this man that his son had cold bloodedly murdered his wife and his colleague and was aided and abetted, in doing so, by Elaine? In truth, he could not and so, at least, he would be spared that. In the final analysis, she had betrayed everything she had stood for and in doing so, had ended up with no options. At least her actions had allowed the whole mess to be covered up by MI5 and the Home office. She and her family had, at least, been left with some dignity.

"We had a strange conversation just before she died." Her husband continued his speech painstakingly slow. "I think she knew that time was running out for her and she wanted to repent in some way? Is that possible?"

In truth, Tim knew that Elaine was aware that he was closing in on his wife's killer, her son. Time was indeed running out for her and her son. If Elaine had not killed her son, Tim would have. Tim, at that time, had been blinded by the need for vengeance and it was her only way out.

"It is wholly possible. You need to believe she did what she had to do. In the end, she did what was best for you, her son, herself and in the ultimate, she did what was best for her Country. You should take comfort that she tried to put matters right."

He looked up very slowly and with difficulty at Tim. There was a look of gratitude in his eyes. He needed something to hold on to, some small part of his wife that would redeem her. He desperately needed to rationalise the death of his only son. Like any father, he only saw the little boy that he had shared time with and nourished. At least, he was to be spared the truth of his son's callous greed and careless disregard for human life.

"She left something for you, in the top left hand drawer, in the desk."

Tim got up, putting his tea down on the coffee table and walked to the desk. He pulled open the drawer to reveal the large buff envelope. It was addressed to him. He took it.

He left the old paralysed man as he had found him, lonely, broken and confused. Tim reflected that had death come sooner to Elaine's husband, he would have been spared the heartbreak he now suffered. It was ironic that his death would have been a better option than living and mourning his wife and only child.

Tim opened the envelope while Harriet sat drinking a can of cola. He pulled the contents out and began to read. The first document surprised him not at all. It was the original documentation that was in the possession of Jeff Stiles, the then Deputy Head of MI5, and his wife. It was the piece of paper that Nicholas Wilkins had killed them for. It was proof that three Russian mobsters were running a massive money laundering and crime funding operation using a fronting bank, the Baltic.

Vasiliev Nikhil, Sokolov Yerik and Volkov Lesta were big time and had links all the way to the Kremlin. Tim stared at the document bearing their signatures. It was enough, along with the evidence that MI5 already held, to allow the Americans to freeze and seize their assets around the World, as part of the sanctions imposed on the Russians following the annexation of the Crimea.

Tim wanted these men dead. It was their threats to Nicholas Wilkins's life that had forced him to kill for them, just to obtain this bit of paper. Ultimately, these three had been responsible for his Wife and Stiles' deaths. Their greed and lust for more had set in train the events that resulted in the whole tragic episode. He would go after these bastards and he would use all the resources at his disposal to do so. Now, as acting head of MI5, he had considerable resources he could use.

He continued through the contents of the envelope. He was staggered. Elaine had not merely kept the evidence her son had taken, but had dug further. Tim realised that she must have had some plan to nullify the power of these men and ultimately free her son from their control. She had been meticulous in her work. Tim realised, she had pulled in every contact she had in her investigation and called in favours from colleagues around the Globe.

There, on the desk, was every detail of every transaction and communication carried out by Nikhil, Yerik and Lesta. He had the goods on them, so to speak. He just needed to pull the trigger and there was enough to lock them up for a long time. In the real world, he knew that would not happen. They would stay in Russia and the authorities would just refuse to extradite them. They would live in luxury, with the only inconvenience being their lack of overseas holidays.

Tim wanted more than that. He wanted them dead.

"Harriet, I want you to follow up on these two names, Mel Levy and Graham Pelham. I want everything on them. I mean everything. I want them sewn up tight. We have come across them before, but now we have this additional information, I want you to dig deep. Follow every thread. I want leverage on these two. We are going after the Russian mobsters. Mel Levy is a corrupt fund manager in the US who works for the Russians. I have meet Graham Pelham. He is a dodgy Isle of Man lawyer, up to his neck in money laundering. Get me everything you can on them. I want enough on them both to send them away for a thousand years."

Chapter 5

The neon sign on the "Tight Lips" nightclub was switched off and wouldn't be illuminated for another seven hours. Moscow was freezing. The sudden early cold snap had caused traffic chaos and all flights in and out of the airport had been suspended. In a Country renowned for its harsh winters, it still lacked the organisation and infrastructure to deal with the inevitable sudden snowfall. Corruption was at the root of the problem. The Mayor and his cronies had their hands in every pie. Funds were siphoned off from every civic project and the Kremlin needed its fair share of the booty.

Proceedings had already started at the Club by the time Lesta made it through the traffic. The roads were always a mess. Driving licences were, in the main, obtained by bribery and not by the taking of a test. The addition of a few millimetres of snow to the mix ensured that the crash rate rocketed as incompetent drivers, in often un-roadworthy cars, bounced into each other like dodgems at a fair ground.

Yerik and Nikhil sat at a table drinking vodka, warming them against the chill as Lesta entered. "Fucking traffic, fucking drivers, fucking Country, fucking bollocks," he said, as he made his way down the steps into the main area of the club, where the stage and the stripper's pole were. He joined his companions at their table.

"And hello to you to," said Nikhil. Lesta noticed that Yerik's hands were heavily bandaged, but he, however, appeared to have no difficulty using them to raise his glass of vodka to his lips.

"What the fuck happened to you?"

"Someone blew my boat up." Yerik had a multi-million pound yacht moored in Monaco.

"The Lady Heloise?" asked Lesta.

"I was in one of the bedrooms when it happened. Most of the crew were not so lucky and were blown to buggery. I was lucky. I just burnt my hands getting off the boat."

"Who did it?" asked Lesta.

"Obviously someone, I pissed off"

"Well that's a fucking long list to choose from," said Nikhil, as he took another swig of vodka. They laughed as Lesta, having removed his fur hat and outer coat, took his seat.

"Seriously what did the police say?"

"After the attacks along the Rivera, they put it down to terrorists, Islamic fundamentalists."

"I go with your motive. Definitely some fucker you screwed over looking to get even."

Their conversation was interrupted by two of Lesta's entourage dragging a semi-conscious, semi-naked man into the room and tying him to the lap-dancing pole in the middle of the stage.

"What's this about?" said Nikhil.

"Oh! Him, he's just some fucking arsehole, who thought he would try and have one over on me," said Lesta, as he waived, for his goons to carry on with their beating of the hapless man.

"What's he been up to?"

"Just a bit of capitalism, it is all the rage now in Russia. He thought he would pimp girls out of my club and not give me my cut. Now, he is just about to make good. Ignore him. He is not the reason for dragging you here."

There was a brief pause in the conversation while they watched the stage show. The man was now blubbering, as they punched him repeatedly." Keep the fucking noise down," said Lesta. "We are trying to talk here."

"So what's it about?"

"It, my friend, is about us losing nearly eight hundred million dollars on the fucking arms deal in Syria. The Kremlin is fucked off. If they don't get their cut, they will remove our concessions and replace us with someone who can deliver, "said Lesta.

"Fuck me! It was their fucking planes that blew the convoy up with our missile launchers on it. Now they are blaming us?"

"They sort of have a point. We were financing the sale of ground to air missiles to ISIS that would have been used to target our own Russian planes."

"Put like that, I suppose it wasn't the best idea." They laughed.

"The bottom line is, we need to make up the losses," said Yerik

The screams were rising from the stage. Lesta gave a warning glance to his men, who shoved a gag in the victim's mouth.

"There is the construction project down the road. You know the new sport and leisure complex. We could try and squeeze that. Should be fifty mill in that, at least."

"Are you fucking mad," said Nikhil. "That's the Mayor of Moscow's wife's build and we don't want to piss her off as well. Anyway, that's already being milked. "

"We need a big deal or we, my friends, will lose our backing and that will be fucking bad for our health. Ideas anyone?"

There was a shaking of heads and blank looks.

The man's screams were rising again. "For fuck's sake," said Nikhil.

He got up walked across the room and stepped onto the stage. He pulled his gun and shot the semi-conscious man in the head.

"Great, that's fucking brilliant. Thanks for nothing. I didn't want the cunt dead. Now I am a man short, have a body to get rid of and a fucking shitty mess all over the stage," said Lesta.

"Well, I couldn't hear myself think with all that racket going on." Nikhil took another slug of vodka as he resumed his seat. "Where were we? "

"We are where we have to get some fucking serious money together to get those that run the Country off our backs, or we will be out of business and probably going for a swim in the river."

Chapter 6

Aleena pulled herself closer to Nizar as the temperature dropped and the rain crashed onto the roof of the old ruin of the farmhouse. Long abandoned, it sat in the middle of a muddy field. The outbuildings were still in use as storage space for farm equipment, but the house served no purpose and had been allowed to fall into disrepair. The Pays de Calais was littered with such buildings, as the old small holdings which would in a bygone age have supported a farming family, were brought up to form larger, modern and more efficient operations. It was November and the farm equipment would not be used for several months. They were safe for the moment.

They had left the Jungle and made their way along the coast in the hope of finding another route into the UK. Their journey from Iraq had been hard and costly. Their money was soon depleted by the people smugglers, who had got them as far as the Jungle camp in Calais. Like so many others, they had been unable to get further. The lack of authority in the Camp had allowed them to exist without detection, but for all intents and purposes, it was little better than a prison. Their choice was stark. Live as vagrants in a virtual prison in France, or face long prison sentences in England as returning terrorists.

Nizar knew that as one of the ISIS leaders in Iraq, his sentence would be very long and there was the danger that he would be charged with murder and war crimes for the atrocities committed by his Jihadis. He also knew that he and Aleena could not continue their current way of life. He knew he was guilty of these things, but it had not meant to be that way. Like many young Muslim men, he had been frustrated by his life in England. Like all young men, he had wanted change and excitement. The preaching of the radical Imams had appealed to his youthful idealism. They had painted a picture of an Islamic State in which their lives would be transformed. It all sounded so idyllic

The reality was a long way from the picture painted after Friday Prayers. At first, they had gained territory. The forces in Iraq were ill prepared to deal with their brutal and swift action. The British and Americans had left Iraq with an ill-prepared and poorly equipped security force. ISIS had gained territory. In Syria, where Assad's army was facing assaults on all fronts by rebel factions, they had found it easy to establish themselves and link their forces in the two Countries.

ISIS had started to rule and form its Caliphate. They had been uncompromising in their application of their version of Islam. Dissenters were executed and strict laws imposed on the population. They had destroyed ancient monuments, considered blasphemous and subjected the population to rape, murder and torture, all in the name of Allah.

Nizar had watched as they became a band of thugs, stealing, raping and murdering. He was in charge, but not in control. He began to hate himself, knew he was on a false path and this was not the true religion that he believed in. It was a corrupt self-serving monster that had become the preserve of sadistic fanatics.

Of course, it could not last. The opposition forces in Iraq gradually became organised and with support from their Allies, led by the US, the tide began to turn. The Kurdish army and the Iraqi forces combined to work together and with allied air support, were now decimating ISIS. They were being driven from the land they had seized. Soon there would be no place for them to hide.

In Syria, the Russians had arrived and mercilessly bombed the rebels. They bombed and they killed. They had no qualms as to their actions. Assad, with their support, would rid the Country of all opposition to his regime. Civilians, ISIS, all and any in opposition would be bombed, shot and starved into submission. ISIS was being left with nowhere to run.

Nizar knew that they would not give up and even if they were defeated in Syria, Iraq and the Yemen, they would fight on. They would bring terror to the streets, cities and homes in the West. Before running from the battle for Mosul, he had set in motion a planned attack on London. It was to be a statement of defiance, to remind the World that they still had teeth and were to be feared. He had personally had enough of the death, murder and misery being carried out in the name of Islam, but he had to see it through. The alternative would have been his torture and death. The terrorist cell was in place, the bombs supplied and the money made available. He had planned it all. He had recruited the suicide bombers, trained them in Syria and sent them to England. He regretted that more deaths would soon follow, but there was nothing he could do to stop it.

Nizar was beginning to drift into sleep as he huddled up to Aleena. The beating of the rain on the roof was rhythmic and soporific. He slipped deeper into sleep, his mind emptying of the cares, horrors past and to come as unconsciousness enveloped him.

With a start, he realised that he and Aleena were no longer alone in the abandoned farmhouse. Years of combat should have enabled him to maintain vigilance, even in sleep, but he had not stirred as the door opened and the figure came in.

He panicked. He struggled awake. He opened his eyes. He froze. The light from the torch blinded him as he woke. As his eyes adjusted, he saw the gun pointing directly at his forehead.

"Got you, you fucker. Don't think of moving," said Adnan.

Chapter 7

Mel Levy had found it difficult to get to his offices, just a quarter of a mile from the New York Stock Exchange. The election of Donald Trump had not been met with universal approval and Times Square was blocked by protestors. To add to the congestion, Christmas shopping was underway and the queues outside Macy's Department Store on Broadway, were adding to the chaos.

He stroked the bronze statue of the Charging Bull in Bowling Green Park, before crossing the road into the Subway food outlet. He grabbed his usual black coffee and sub and finally made it to the lobby of the building. The doors opened automatically and he crossed the atrium to the security check, holding his identity pass and food in one hand and his briefcase in the other.

The guard, who usually greeted him with a friendly smile before waving him through, stopped him. "Pass."

"Err, it's me Jim. Like, the me, you have let in for the last year or so."

Jim ignored Mel and took the pass from his hand. Instead of returning it and waving him through, he raised his hand in the air holding the pass aloft.

Mel was startled by the sudden appearance of the two men. "Come with us." He was positioned between them and both his arms were held in a firm and unyielding grip. He was frogmarched to the exit. He started to resist. "I would not do that if I were you,

Mr Levy," said one.

The black car pulled up as they stepped onto the sidewalk. The doors opened and he was pushed onto the back seat where a further intimidating figure already sat. One of his abductors followed him on to the back seat. He was now flanked on either side. His other abductor walked to the front of the car and sat beside the driver.

"Who are you? Where are you taking me?"

There was no response. He felt fear and panic. Mel knew he had done some pretty dodger things in his time on Wall Street and had spent four years in prison in recompense. He was always dealing with crooks and drug smugglers in his daily activities laundering their money, but he was fairly sure that he had displeased none of them.

He shouted, "Who are you?"

"Shut the fuck up. We are not going to kill you. We are just taking you to meet someone."

They pulled up outside the Waldorf Astoria, where he and the three men got out the car before it drove off. As they stood on the moving sidewalk taking them to the main lobby, he considered running. "Calm down, if we were going to harm you we would hardly take you to a hotel. Would we?"

They passed the iconic art deco clock in the reception area and headed to the lifts that would take them to the Waldorf Tower rooms. They rode in silence to the top floor. He was escorted from the elevator along the corridor. The door to the suite was opened. He was pushed inside and the door closed behind him. He stood for a moment looking into the room. On the couch, a figure was seated, drinking a cup of tea.

"Come in Mr Levy, I should like to talk with you." Tim Burr took another sip of tea as he waived for his guest to sit down in the chair opposite.

****

The Island had been hit by the first of the winter storms the previous night. Roof tiles had been lifted, drains blocked and bins scattered around the streets. The seagulls had started the clean up by descending on the overturned bins, ripping the refuse sacks to pieces and picking over their contents for anything they could eat. The Isle of Man never really experienced snow and ice, but sat in the sea between Liverpool, on the UK mainland and Ireland, it did get a lot of wind and rain.

Graham Pelham parked his car in the multi story car park and walked up Athol Street to his office. The outside of the Advocate's office, the entrance lobby and stairwell were festooned with brass plaques. Each had the name of a company engraved upon it. Graham made his money by setting up and running shell companies that helped his clients avoid any tax, anytime, anywhere. He put his umbrella in the stand and removed his coat, shaking the moisture from it before hanging it up.

He was early and his secretary had not yet arrived. He opened the door to his office and was surprised to see a young woman occupying his seat.

"Can I help you?" his voice was confrontational.

"It's more the other way round. I am here to help you." Harriet Shaw, Tim's assistant, replied calmly.

"I have no idea who you are, or who you think you are, but I want you to leave right now."

"Please sit down. I am from MI5. The head of MI5, Mr Burr has asked me to talk with you."

34

He sat. He knew Tim. Their connection had been an international assassin known as Annubis. He had hoped that the matter was dead and buried to their mutual benefit. He was acutely aware that MI5 could make his life acutely uncomfortable. He gestured for the young woman to continue.

"Mr Burr requires your assistance in a matter."

"I am not sure I want to get involved in MI5 matters."

"It is not a request." She pushed a file across the desk. He sat and opened the file. They sat in silence as he read. He eventually looked up visibly shaken.

"I don't understand?"

"It is quite simple Mr Pelham. I have been digging into a number of transactions involving you, Mr Levy and three Russians, called Yerik, Nikhil and Lesta. You don't deny knowing and doing business with these people do you?"

Graham sat silently, unsure how to respond. His brain raced, but he could not see why a bit of tax dodging would interest MI5. "I know these people. They are clients, yes but ...."

"Let me stop you there. They are not clients. They are international terrorists..."

"They are businessmen. That is all." He interrupted in his turn.

"The three Russians, aided and abetted by you and Mel Levy, put together a financial package early last month. The sum involved was over half a billion US Dollars. This money was to be used to purchases missiles for ISIS, to be used against Allied forces, including British planes. Do you understand now Mr Pelham?"

He was flustered and his stomach knotted in fear." I knew nothing of this."

"This is not a case of your bending the rules and doing a bit of speculative and creative accounting to help the rich avoid their tax. We view this as you sponsoring and facilitating terrorism. This is not a rap over the knuckles and a fine. You are looking at a court case in camera and twenty years behind bars."

The colour drained from Pelham's face and he felt sick with fear. He began to tremble and looked at Harriet pleadingly.

"Calm down, we are only talking at the moment. Of course, if our chat it not satisfactory, I think matters would progress rapidly and you should prepare yourself for a visit from Special Branch. Do you follow me?"

He nodded.

"Mr Burr would like you to come to Thames House in London, where in return for our not releasing this file, he would like your full and complete co-operation in a matter close to his heart. I therefore ask you, if you are willing to cooperate fully and unquestioningly with MI5, to combat these terrorists?"

****

Tim was sat in the lobby of the Waldorf Hotel with a senior official from Homeland Security. "Thank you for putting the frighteners on Mr Levy and bringing him here."

"We should arrest Levy you know," said the official

"Technically, he has been involved in financing terrorism, but he is only small fry. I want the Russian scumbags. I know you have enough to charge them and take them to trial. We both know that will not happen. There is not a cat in hells chance the Kremlin will extradite them to the States. You will just end up with Mel, who is little more than a petty hustler scraping around for a living," said Tim.

"So, we let Mr Levy walk?"

"No you let him fly to the UK, where I will use him to get those Russian bastards, to break cover and where they are vulnerable. Outside of Russia we can nail them," said Tim.

Chapter 8

Nikhil decided he would drive himself as he woke to a crisp, dry day in his villa, on the outskirts of St Petersburg. Moscow had still been a slushy mess when he had left. The snow had stopped, but the temperature was still low enough to keep the remnants clinging to the sidewalks and allow the roads to turn to ice overnight. Red Square was, however, completely pristine. An army of elderly women with snow shovels, little more than a large piece of plywood nailed to a broom handle, had been deployed to clear it. Nikhil wondered where these women appeared from, but they did, every time it snowed.

It was mid-morning by the time he got into his Aston Martin DB9. He had a small fleet of cars, but this was by far his favourite. The external temperature was still just above freezing and he revved the engine a few times to warm it. In truth, he just liked the sound of the exhaust note growling angrily, as he pressed the throttle. It was just past ten as he drove down his driveway and out onto the road. He hoped that most of the traffic would have cleared and he would get a clear run. It would be nice to put his foot down and feel the power of the car as it roared along.

The first leg of his journey did not allow him to explore the cars capability. The road from his villa was narrow and twisty. In many ways, Russia had come a long way since the fall of Communism. In other ways, it had stood still. The rich were very rich, but the poor were very poor and going backwards. Outside of the major centres, life was little changed. The rural communities struggled. The young left for the cities looking to chase their dreams, leaving the old and infirm behind.

In Moscow and St Petersburg the new rich could be seen in their finery, driving their luxury imported cars, but in the backwaters of economic stagnation, there was little progress. Nikhil kept his speed down as he drove through the village with its wooden buildings and their steep roofs. He was aware that he could still encounter a car driven by a local that would belch smoke and travel haphazardly at ten or twelve miles an hour.

Finally, he reached the highway and putting his foot down, he listened as the Aston surged forward with a satisfying growl, unleashing its five hundred-horse power. He ignored the speed limit and like a young boy racer, he pushed the car to perform.

He saw the waiting police cars. He smiled. It was a Friday. He had forgotten. Friday was payday. It was like a tax the police imposed on motorists. Their salaries were ridiculously low and they supplemented them by various acts of bribery and corruption. Friday was their day to fleece motorist, so they had sufficient cash to see them over the weekend. It was the system and the motorists went along with it, knowing if they didn't pay up, life would become a whole lot more difficult for them.

"Morning officer Kerov," smiled Nikhil, as he reached into his pocket to retrieve his wallet.

The policeman did not return his greeting, or smile. This was odd as they had gone through this ritual countless times before. "Do you realise that you were doing twice the speed limit Sir?"

"Sorry officer." Nikhil found his wallet and offered the customary bribe.

"What is that? You do realise it is an offence to attempt to bribe an officer of the law?"

Nikhil was astounded. This never happened before. He had

bribed this officer countless times. Kerov began to write the ticket requiring Nikhil to present himself for further enquiries. He was not even to be given an official on the spot fine.

The officer lent into the car and gave him the ticket. He mouthed silently to Nikhil as he handed it to him. "Sorry, it has come down from the top."

Nikhil got the message. They had better make good the loss of the failed arms deal or life was going to get very uncomfortable for him.

****

The Tight Lips was just about to open its doors in Moscow. It was ten in the evening. There were few punters, owing to the weather and the girls were earning very little as they stripped with little enthusiasm. Their money came from the private lap dances. The client would be taken to a back room where the girls would perform. Unlike the clubs in the US, extras were available and touching was encouraged.

Lesta was just about to leave when he heard a commotion from the lobby. The bouncers were usually more than capable of dealing with any resistance from the punters the club fleeced, so Lesta was surprised.

He made his way to the entrance. He was confronted in the lobby, crowded with police and officials. "What the fuck is going on?" he demanded. This did not happen. He paid the requisite bribes to all the relevant people regularly and they left him alone. Now the place was teeming with government minions.

"Fire and licensing, we are here to inspect."

Lesta could hardly believe it as the club was mobbed by officials and the punters ushered from the premises. He knew it was a set up. The club would be closed. The paper work had already been prepared, the inspection, merely a bit of theatrics.

He was handed the notice and they left. He had the message loud and clear." Sort it, or suffer the consequences."

****

Yerik had not been forgotten as the Kremlin sought to focus the oligarchs' attentions on their obligation to make restitution for the losses they had incurred.

The dawn raid on his aluminium factory had brought it to a halt. Taxation was, in the main, a voluntary exercise for the favoured in Russia. Tax was, in effect, the bribes paid to the various officials and not an obligatory payment to the State Treasury. It was, however, a means by which the Kremlin would seek to get one returned to Russia, if they moved abroad and criticised the administration. Many an exiled Russian soon found, that as soon as they spoke out against Mother Russia, they would be the subject of extradition proceedings, accused of tax evasion and corruption. If they were unfortunate to be extradited, then they were stripped of everything and banged up for ever. The State did not like critics.

Yerik had not criticised the State, but he, Lesta and Nikhil, had lost money. This was bad, if not worse. He knew they were all on notice.

"Pay up or suffer the consequences".

Chapter 9

Jimmy Buari was driving to the location of the dead drop. It was not a long drive, or at least it should not have been. A pile up on the M1 had caused chaos on all the surrounding roads in the area. Everyone travelling south in the morning rush to work had the same idea. Get off the motorway at Luton and head cross country using the minor roads to get to work.

Jimmy was stuck in stagnant traffic just before Wheathampsted. He was trying to make his way towards the Great North Wood near Cuffley, in Hertfordshire. He knew the journey well. He and Nizar had often come to the woods when they were at the University in Hatfield. Apart from the Galleria Shopping Centre, the town itself was run down and offered very little entertainment. Being Muslims, the main student pastime, of getting blind drunk, had not been an option. They and their mates would, however, smoke dope in the woods. They had their favourite spot hidden off the beaten track, where they would gather in the summer and get high.

He and Nizar had shared a flat in Luton after they finished their university course. Luton had a large Muslim population, mostly of Pakistani origin. Jimmy was of Nigerian descent and being black, was at first viewed with some suspicion at the Mosque. As time went by, however, Nizar and he became fully integrated into the community as a whole. They attended the Mosque regularly and following Nizar's lead, joined a study group.

Over time, their opinions had become more hard-line, more extreme and more fundamental. It had been a slow process. A combination of factors slowly led them down that path. A mix of biased policing, racism and lack of money hardened both their views. Gradually they developed an idealised view of the perfect Islamic society, a society in which they could see themselves living.

Jimmy could still feel the excitement the day they had set out for the training camp in Pakistan. While Nizar travelled directly, Jimmy had first gone to Nigeria, before travelling on. That decision, to stop off in Nigeria, had been where their fortunes had diverged.

Nizar was on the terrorist watch list and would have been arrested on returning to the UK. Jimmy, having flown out and back via Nigeria, slipped under the radar and returned without raising any flags. Nizar had gone on to Iraq and Syria and had become a high raking commander in ISIS. Jimmy had come back and established a number of cells in the UK. Nizar was Jimmy's controller. Targets were set by ISIS and Nizar would instruct and coordinate the various individual cells across the UK, Each cell operated in isolation. They had no knowledge of other groups of terrorists and so, if caught, could not betray them.

One group would acquire a part of the material necessary to make a bomb and another group other parts so as to not arouse suspicion. The materials would be left at various locations and collected by another group. None would meet. The bomb would be assembled and stored. The bombers would then be directed to collect the bomb and instructed in their target. Nizar was the coordinator and Jimmy took his instructions from him.

Jimmy finally pulled into the car park of the Wood. It was a pay car park, but the hut by the entrance was not open yet, so he drove straight in. He parked the car and taking his Wellington boots from the boot of the car, put them on. Following the rain the previous evening, the ground was boggy and he would need them.

The trees were bare of leaves, but the ferns were still green and thick surrounding the tracks through the wood. He stopped on a few occasions, but apart from the odd dog walker, there was no one around. Sure that he was alone, he made his way to the spot where they used to come to smoke weed. Despite the undergrowth having grown back, he easily recognised their old den, hidden in the shrub. The rotting trees stump was still there. It had been there since nineteen eighty-eight, when the hurricane that struck Britain, brought devastation to so many trees. It was slowly rotting and would eventually be reclaimed by the forest as the new trees grew.

The package was inside a plastic supermarket bag to protect the contents from the damp. He retrieved it and made his way back to his car. He put his Wellingtons in the boot and swapped his footwear.

The drive back to Luton against the rush hour traffic was quicker. As he pulled into the road, where he was staying in a converted flat, he was pleased to see he would be able to park almost outside the building. A large proportion of the other residents in the street had taken their cars to drive to work, or the station. The area was predominantly Asian and the shops reflected this.

Closing the door behind him, he made his way to the sitting room. His hands were trembling as he removed his coat and threw it onto the sofa. He pulled out a chair and sat at the dining table that was in the corner of the room, off the galley kitchen. He sat looking at the plastic bag for several seconds, before removing the thick, brown, bubble pack envelope.

Jimmy knew this was it. He had asked for this. He needed to be more than a bystander. He needed to do. He wanted to make his mark. He wanted a legacy. He wanted martyrdom. Now his time had come.

Nizar had been reluctant. Jimmy had been persistent. Nizar had seen enough of death. Jimmy was eager for glory. Nizar saw no glory in the fight anymore, just butchery. Jimmy wanted Jihad, Nizar wanted it to stop. The rape, the murder of innocents and the deaths of young men. ISIS was losing in Syria and in Iraq. Nizar had wanted to come home. Jimmy wanted paradise after death. Jimmy got his way.

He emptied the contents onto the Ikea table. There was a mobile phone, a note and a padlock key. The note gave the address of a self-storage unit and the entry code. The key would unlock the storage unit, that contained the bomb, made and put there by another terrorist cell. The phone was unregistered. Nizar would phone him with his target, the when, the where and the how.

Jimmy's heart was racing and his hands shook. Soon he thought. Soon the whole World would hear of Jimmy Buari

Chapter 10

Nizar started to tremble uncontrollably, as he stared at the gun Adnan was holding inches from his face. In the First World War, they would have recognised it as shell shock. The continuous pounding of the enemy's shells in the trenches, where the soldiers were sheltering, gave the condition its name. After the Gulf war, it became known as Gulf war syndrome. Following more wars and engagements, it got its full name of posttraumatic stress syndrome. People reacted differently to stress, but living day to day in combat conditions, with death as a companion, placed individuals in a constant state of tension. Nizar had gradually broken down in Iraq and Syria.

"What the fuck is the matter with you?" Adnan had been with Nizar in Iraq. He had been on the same journey as Nizar. From England, to the training camps, to the front line, fighting to establish the caliphate. He and Nizar had worked together. Adnan had been placed in charge of procuring the ordinance, the guns and bullets needed to prosecute the ISIS advance. Together they had nearly pulled off the biggest stunt of the war. Between them, they had organised acquiring BUK ground to air missiles. It would have been a game changer in Syria. If they had been successful, ISIS would have had the capability to take down Russian and Allied Jet fighters. Without air power, the Iraqis and the Syrians would have been unable to have driven ISIS out of the territory they had seized.

Looking at Nizar now, huddled in front of him, shaking, Adnan hardly recognised the commander he had fought along side for all those years.

"I just had enough."

Adnan was disgusted. "Our brothers are still dying, fighting Kafirs and you sit cuddling a whore while they die."

Aleena sat rigid, looking at Adnan, as he pointed the gun at her. She had seen him before in the camps and she knew that he could be ruthless. She knew that he would kill them both without hesitation.

"I am tired of the killing, the murder, the rape and the cause. I have beheaded men for having a cell phone, bombed hospitals and watched children blown to bits. I have used fellow Muslims as human shields. I wonder if I am still human."

"It is war. Do you think Assad, the Kurds, the Russians or the Americans give a fuck about who they kill? They have been killing us and using us since the fucking Crusades. They have been murdering us for centuries. They will never stop."

Nizar said nothing. He had enough of the rhetoric, the death and the destruction.

"Did you think you could just abandon your duty? Just pack your bags and go home? Did you really think that you could, just walk away? Leave your brothers to fight and die, without a second thought? Well did you?" Adnan's voice was raised in anger, his frustration growing.

"I didn't think. I saw Aleena being rapeed and something snapped in me. I didn't think, or plan, or anything. I just did. I had enough, that's all. I had enough of the whole fucking shit storm. That's all. I just didn't want to be part of it anymore, no thought, and no plan, just go."

Adnan pulled the cable ties from his pocket. "Put your hands out." He secured Nizar's hands and feet. He then bound Aleena in the same manner. Satisfied that they could not move and posed no

47

further threat, he took his mobile phone from his pocket.

"I have gone through a great deal of trouble catching up with you. That effort will not be wasted. You and your whore will be an example to all those that would betray us." He began filming.

"These are the betrayers. These are the deserters. These are..." He intoned his voice over the video.

He paused the recording and from his pack, he pulled out a large serrated knife, about ten inches in length. He wedged the phone on his pack and checking that he had Aleena and Nizar in shot, he resumed his commentary. "This is the knife that will send our enemies to hell."

Almost chanting he made his way round behind the pair. "I beg you," said Nizar. "Let the girl be. She is only fifteen. She can still have a life."

"Allah is great," was the only repetitive response, he could illicit from Adnan, as he pulled Nizar's head back, exposing his throat.

Nizar knew that it would end this way. He knew from the beginning, when he left England that it would always end this way. Then he had felt the passion, the fervour, the spirit of righteousness. Now, as his death was imminent, the fervour, the religious zeal had evaporated, leaving only the feeling of futility. So much death, so much pain, so much destruction and so little fulfilment at the end, just self doubt and despair.

Time seem suspended. Nizar could hear his own heart racing in his chest. He heard Aleena take a sharp breath and hold it, not breathing out. The gasp you hear from the crowd at a Circus, when the man on the high wire stumbles. He was amazingly calm. He had seen many die in this exact way. He had wondered how he would behave. Most had died without a struggle. Now he knew why. When the hope was gone, the mind accepted that soon the spirit would return to where it had come. Nizar was going home. Going to be with his God and the path all must eventually accept and follow.

Adnan's face was contorted with a religious fever. His eyes were blazing and he was almost in a state of ecstasy as he drew the knife back, preparing to slaughter his sacrifice. He voice had risen to a scream. "Allah is good, Allah is good," he shouted.

Nizar closed his eyes and waited for death to come.

Chapter 11

"You guests are waiting for you," said Harriet, as she popped her head round the door to Tim's office, in MI5's headquarters on the top floor of Thames House.

"I won't be a sec. Go down and wait for me with them."

It had been with some reluctance that Mel Levy, the Wall Street wheeler-dealer, had boarded a plan for the UK, but his choices had been limited. Facing potential terrorist charges, he saw sense and agreed to cooperate. Graham Pelham was also less than keen, but had taken the plane from the Isle of Man to Gatwick that morning. Both now awaited Tim's presence Tim doubled checked, he had all the bits and pieces he would need for the meeting and reassured, he gathered up his files and made his way along the corridor to his meeting.

As Tim entered the room, he was aware of the tension. There was a general air of nervousness. The occupants had their gaze firmly fixed on him, observing his every move and trying to glean something from his body language. The tension was even rubbing off on Harriet. There had been no need to have her present. He knew that he should have had his deputy Harry Denham present, but he had conveniently opted for one of the most junior members of staff in his stead.

Harry had been with MI5 for nearly forty years. His selection had been deliberated. He was there to counter balance Tim's lack of experience. Tim had been given the job for one reason only. He knew too much, too much about the previous head Elaine Wilkins and her betrayal of the Service and her Country. He knew too much about Mailer, the Foreign Secretary and his sordid past. He knew too much about senior members of the establishment and the government.

Tim was head of MI5, not because of what he knew about National Security, but what he knew about the people in power. His promotion was their way of keeping him in check and quiet. Harry Denham was there to control him and report back to the powers that ran the Country. It suited Tim. Harry did what had to be done. Tim did what he wanted to do. What he wanted to do was get justice for his murdered wife.

Her immediate killer was dead, the triggerman who had shot her. Now he wanted the men who had been ultimately responsible for her death. These men were, Vasiliev Nikhil, Sokolov Yerik and Volkov Lesta. The Russian scum, whose greed and lack of any form of morality, had set in train the series of events that had led to his wife's brains being blown out on a hotel veranda in Crete.

Sat in this room were the two men who had direct access to the three Russians. He had them. They were his, to do with as he wanted. If they did not give him what he wanted, they knew they would never leave prison in their lifetimes. He was their only hope of living out their lives outside prison walls.

Harry Denham's absence suited him. He had deliberately picked a general meeting room with no audio or video recording equipment installed. He had made sure he only had a junior officer, whom he could control, present. He was set to deal with the men before him, in total confidence.

"Gentleman, are you comfortable? Does anyone want anything, coffee or tea?" They shook they heads and sat waiting, for him to begin in silence.

He commenced by fixing his gaze on Graham Pelham, the Manx lawyer. "It is nice to see you again." Their paths had crossed previously when Pelham had reason to contact Tim for a client, a somewhat dubious client, who went by the alias of Annubis. The matter had been resolved to both their benefit. That was in the past and now the circumstances had changed.

"And it is nice to meet you Mr Levy," he turned his attention to the moneyman, for the Russians.

Addressing both, he continued. "I am interested in three individuals with whom you are both intimately acquainted. Vasiliev Nikhil, Sokolov Yerik and Volkov Lesta are their names. I need you two gentlemen to help me bring them to justice. Before I continue, I should like you to read the files that I am putting in front of you, one each."

Tim pushed the files across the table to Levy and Pelham. There was silence as they turned pages and read. Their faces became increasingly concerned the more they studied the paperwork. At one point, Levy even let out a gasp. Pelham, with his lawyer training, had more control and read in silence. They looked up at Tim, ashen faced and waited for him to speak.

Tim allowed the tension to build before breaking the silence. "As you can see, you are, what we call in the spy trade, completely fucked. You both helped in the funding of a plot, by our Russian friends, to supply arms to ISIS. Not a few guns, but ground to air missile systems that would potentially have altered affairs in Syria and Iraq."

They both started to protest. "Shut up," said Tim, putting his hands up to silence them. "I am not going to argue legalities and all that malarkey with you. Just shut up and listen. I am only interested in these Russian wankers. You have a choice and you need to make it now. Help me, or I will do everything and use every resource I have to fuck you until hell freezes over. Are you hearing me?

They were shocked into silence. Harriet went to speak, but a warning glance from Tim brought her to silence. He waited in silence. He needed their one hundred per cent cooperation. They needed to be broken. They needed to be in his control. He waited as they contemplated both the evidence against them and Tim's intransigence.

"Well?"

They both acquiesced, their heads bowed. They knew there was no option, but to fully cooperate with this man. Tim having showed them the stick, now produced the carrot. He took two envelopes from the papers in front of him and handed them to the men opposite.

"If you do as I want, I can keep you out of jail. For you Mr Levy is a letter, signed by your US Attorney General, granting you immunity from prosecution, which you will get to keep if I am satisfied with your level of help. For you Mr Pelham, there is a letter, as you can see, signed by me stating you were operating under the orders of MI5 in the interest of National Security, which you will also get to keep if I am happy? You both have "get out of jail free cards" in your hands gentleman."

"Harriet, take the letters back and look after them will you?"

Tim paused briefly as the tension eased in the two men. What I need you two to do is quite simple really. The three men I want are in Russia. There they are protected, unassailable and immune from international law. We have enough to lock them up and throw away the key, but they will never stand trial in the West. Russia will never grant their extradition to face charges. I want those bastards and I want them badly. Gentlemen, you are going to get them for me."

He paused, to be sure they understood how personal the matter was to him. "If you want to save your own backsides, you will get me these bastards. You will get them to leave Russia and come to the UK."

Levy was the first to respond, "Why would they come?"

"Money, they are in trouble. They need to make good some losses to their political masters. They are under pressure in the Motherland to come up with the goods."

Graham and Levy looked at each other. "We will get them to the UK for you."

Chapter 12

Charlie Wicks was eighty-seven today. It was much the same as any other day. He had managed, after a struggle, to get dressed and get into his wheelchair. His wife had died nearly fifteen years ago, but he still missed having her around. He had a daughter, but she, her husband and two children lived in Toronto in Canada. He had not seen the younger of his two grand children, a girl. He used to be able to manage the flight until two years ago. However, when he lost his legs, through diabetes, that option was no longer open to him. He hoped that his daughter would keep her promise and come to England for Christmas with her husband and children.

He heard the clatter of the front door letterbox telling him the postman had made a delivery. Charlie did not usually make the effort to retrieve the post himself. Manoeuvring the wheel chair to the front door was difficult. He had not wanted to move to a new, more wheelchair friendly flat. This was the house his wife and he had bought when they first married. He had raised his daughter here. He wife had died here, in her home. There were too many memories to move.

Today, being his birthday, he decided to go through the rigmarole necessary to get himself to the front door. There was a prospect of a birthday card from his grandchildren on offer, that would make the effort worthwhile he decided.

The journey to his front door proved arduous, time consuming and disappointing. There was no card, just a typed letter. He retrieved it and began the journey back to his living room, where he would wait for his daily visit from his carer.

His living room was heavily adorned with memorabilia from his stint in the Royal Air Force. There was a painting of the Spitfire fighters, flying over the White Cliffs of Dover during the Battle of Britain in World War II. A model of a Lancaster Bomber, he had assembled and painted, from an Airfix kit sat above the mantelpiece. There was a small display case with a glass font that contained his service medals on the wall.

Charlie had been in the RAF, not a pilot, but ground crew. With hindsight, it had been good times. As a young man, it had all been a big adventure, away from home, comrades and foreign travel. He had been a child during the Second World War. He and his parents had lived in London. He had been sent to stay with a family in Kent while the blitz raged over the docks in the East End, where his parents remained. His father was not conscripted, as he was needed as a worker on the docks.

After the War, he had moved back to the East End and when old enough, he had joined the Air Force and was sent to Aden. Nothing seemed to have changed to Charlie as he watched the news. The strife in the Yemen continued. The Arabs had been killing one another when the British were there and now they will still killing one another with the help of the Saudis and the Iranians.

Leaving the RAF, he had met his wife and they had moved to a new build Council House in Kent. He had always wanted to move back to Kent, as he had fond memories of the countryside as an evacuee as a child. When Prime Minister Thatcher had introduced the right to buy your council house, they had snapped up the opportunity. He loved the house and wanted to stay till he died.

"Hello," he heard Sinita call, as she opened the door.

He responded and she appeared at the door of the living room. She came in twice a day to help him. "Have you had breakfast?"

Charlie admitted he had not, so she went to the kitchen and began clattering around, clearing and washing the previous evenings plates and boiling the kettle. She reappeared about fifteen minutes later, with toast and tea for him and tea for herself. She sat and spoke with him as he ate.

He appreciated that she was spending her own time to talk to him. The time she was paid for, by the Council, would in reality be sufficient to do half the work that needed doing, but she did it and found time to converse with him.

She wore the hijab to cover her head, which Charlie was very familiar with, having spent so long in a Muslim Country. Charlie enjoyed her company and she was always friendly and seemed genuinely interested in his life and in particular, his association with the RAF.

"Tell me," she said. "Are you all set to go on parade in two weeks?"

Charlie had forgotten all about Remembrance Sunday. When his wife had passed away, he had attempted to not become isolated, so he sought out and joined in the RAF association. They met, reminisced and went on parade. He had the honour of being the standard-bearer, until he lost his legs, but he was still collected by them to attend meetings and get-togethers. He had been on parade before at the Cenotaph in Whitehall and was waiting to see if transport could be arranged, so he would be able to parade with his regiment this year.

"The letter, I forgot," he pointed to the letter that had arrived earlier on the mantelpiece. "Get it would you?"

She walked over and retrieved it. "Open it for me and read what it says. I can't be bothered to retrieve my specs," he said.

She examined the envelope and making sure not to tear it, carefully pulled open the flap and pulled out the letter. She began, "Dear Mr Wicks, we have organised transport to collect you at

57

seven thirty on Remembrance Sunday and take you to the assembly point." The letter continued, with details of marching order, times and location.

"That is brilliant." She said, "I shall watch on the television and look out for you."

"Would you take my blazer to the dry cleaners for me and my blue overcoat, I best polish my medals hadn't I," he joked.

"I think your wheelchair may be more the issue. I am not sure it is up to the job?"

"I've been onto them, but no response. I am on the waiting list for a new one, but, who knows."

"Can you possibly manage without it for a few days? I know that it will be a nuisance, but perhaps something could be done."

"I don't have much money and these things are extortionate."

"I have a friend who mends bikes and things. I could ask him if he can do anything. It has to be worth ago."

Charlie was really grateful. Over past few weeks the left wheel had seemed to become gradually looser after each of Sinita's visits. "Thank you. You are so kind"

****

"Well?" said Jimmy Buari, when Sinita returned to the flat they shared.

"He is on parade and he has agreed to you collecting his wheelchair. He had little choice, if I loosened the wheel nuts anymore they would drop off if you just looked at it," she laughed.

"And who could resist the Rolls Royce of wheelchairs. I will return to him as a gift?" He gestured to the brand new wheelchair he had purchased that sat in the corner of the lounge.

All Jimmy needed now was a phone call from Nizar confirming the target and he would go ahead and load Charlie's new wheelchair with the bomb. He had already set up the remote detonation using a mobile phone. Just dial the number and it will explode.

Chapter 13

Adnan chanting was silenced by the sound of a single shot. Aleena let out a load scream as a red dot appeared on his forehead. The shot was inch perfect and death was instantaneous. The knife slipped from his hand and he toppled to the side, dead before he hit the ground.

Nizar opened his eyes and could barely comprehend that he was still alive. Save for the sound of the rain beating on the roof of the abandoned building, there was silence. Aleena sat frozen, mouth opened and the scream stifled. She stared beyond Nizar, beyond the dead body of Adnan, at the rain soaked figure standing in the doorway.

Rafiq, the man from MI5 had followed Nizar and Aleena from the camp. He knew that they were not right, not refugees and obviously, British. He suspected them to be terrorists. They were trying to get back unobserved into the UK. He had tracked them from the jungle to the derelict farmhouse.

It was clear they were going to ground there, so he had left, made his way to the local town and had dinner at the local café. He negotiated with the patron for a room for the night.

He had had a shower. He had a few hours sleep and changed his clothes. Refreshed, he had made his way back to the farm on the edge of town at around four in the morning. He stealthily approached the building to verify that the two suspects were still present and sleeping. Instead of finding two sleeping suspects he had, peering through the window, seen a knife wielding homicidal maniac and his two suspects bound and awaiting execution.

Rafiq was fit and he was trained, but he was also unarmed. He did not fancy his chances of tackling the gun and knife carrying Adnan. He was in a dilemma. He had his mobile, but he knew by the time he managed to convince the local gendarmes of who he was and what was happening, it would clearly be too late for the two captives.

He could do little and needed to bide his time until the opportunity arose for further action on his part. He watched as Adnan ranted at the tied Nizar. He watched as Adnan drew the big serrated knife. He watched as Adnan put the gun down and approached Nizar with the intention of decapitating him. Then Rafiq moved.

The door was not locked in anyway and was barely shut. Rafiq took a deep breech and swiftly made his move. He knew he only had the one opportunity and he needed to do it right, or he could well end up being the third body found in the derelict building.

He rushed the door, which gave easily and flew open. He focussed on the gun and raced towards it. He checked the safety was off and in one move aimed and fired. One thing he had excelled in in training was shooting. He was smooth and accurate and Adnan died.

Standing with the gun in his hand, Rafiq took a second deep breath and calmed himself after the adrenaline rush of the split second action that had proceeded the moment.

"That was close," said Rafiq. "Now, tell me, who you two are?" He was surprised how calm his voice sounded, given the circumstances.

Nizar was, however, far from calm and was shaking uncontrollably. Aleena was frozen in fear. There was silence in

61

response.

"For fucks sake, somebody say something. I am not here for my health you know."

Nizar finally composed himself and spoke." Who are you?"

"I think you'll find you are not in a position to ask the questions. I suggest you answer mine. I can tell you are British and I am guessing you have been a very naughty boy in Syria or Iraq. So just give me your name."

Aleena looked at Nizar and broke the silence. "I just want to go home to Walsall," she said simply.

Rafiq saw a young frightened girl and responded. "Don't worry, you'll be OK." He looked at Nizar and waited. There was no response.

Rafiq removed his cell phone from his pocket and started to dial.

Nizar, roused himself, panicked. "Who are you calling?"

"The police, what do you expect. I have a dead man and a suspected terrorist. What do you think, I should do?"

"Just wait, you are from MI5?" Rafiq nodded and did not press the connect button on the phone as Nizar spoke. "I am, I was the regional commander of the ISIS forces in Mosul. My name is Nizar Mirza."

Rafiq was taken aback at Nizar's revelation and took a moment to consider. He had little in the way of options open to him. He knew that the intelligence service would want to question this man and they would want to do it quietly. He could be invaluable to them as a source of intelligence. There was the problem of him being in farmhouse in the middle of the French countryside. He had little choice but to call the French anti-terror forces and hand him over.

He looked down at his phone and he pressed the dial button.

"Stop," Nizar was almost pleading. "I want to come home. I want to get Alana home. I have something to trade."

Rafiq pressed the disconnect button on the phone." I am listening."

"There is a plot, I have the details and more. I can give you half the terrorist living and hiding in England. I was the co-ordinator for ISIS on the UK terror campaign. I want to trade immunity for Aleena and I will give it all up to MI5."

Rafiq knew the importance of the information, but he did not have the means to get Aleena and Nizar back to the UK and Thames House.

"I will come with you voluntarily. Just get us back into the UK. I am sick of the killing and death. I just want out. Get me home."

Rafiq made the decision. He hoped to God he had made the right one. He walked across the room and picked up the knife Adnan had been set to use. He cut the cable ties and set Nizar and Aleena free. He put the gun in his pocket.

"Get your stuff together. Let's find breakfast and a hotel. We'll sort it from there."

Chapter 14

The hot topic on everyone's lips was the US Presidential Election and Thames House was no different. The race between Hilary Clinton and Donald Trump, Democrat and Republican nominees respectively, was gripping the US. Neither candidate was popular, but they were the choices available. Tim was looking at the latest assessments. With three weeks to the election, on the eighth of November, Clinton seemed to be the clear favourite to win. The FBI had cleared her of wrongdoing, despite having used an unauthorized server to send and receive emails, whilst in office as Secretary of State. Earlier in the year, in March, thousands of her emails had been leaked to the media.

"What do you make of the Presidential campaign?" He asked Denham.

"Unbelievable, the only good part is, that it should give the tossers at the Foreign Office a pile of crap to deal with. If Trump gets in, they won't know their arse from their tits."

"You are right, there is always an upside to everything," laughed Tim. "What's next on this morning's agenda?"

"Levy and Pelham are back and waiting to see you."

"OK, send them in and I want you to look into that attempted cyber hack on the Department of Health. Number 10 is unhappy that it is being undermined by the French with their Brexit negotiations. They are trying to look strong on Foreigners using the system and that latest hack is not helping one jot."

"Ok, will do." Denham got up and left. After a few moments, Pelham and Levy were sat in the chairs on the opposite side of Tim's desk.

"Well, have you come up with a plan to get Yerik, Nikhil and Lesta within our reach?"

"It is not that easy," said Levy.

"I am disappointed, but you are the one's facing the jail time, not me. So, I am also surprised."

"We do have something," said Pelham hastily. "It is not financial. I don't think we could find anything attractive enough to get them to risk leaving Russia. It would have to be in the billion dollar range and that sort of scam is not done overnight,"

"Well, tell me. What exactly do you have? It had better be good?" said Tim.

"There is big money to be made betting on Trump to win and become the President," said Levy

"Well that's not going to happen. Clinton is a ninety-two per cent favourite. I have just been reading a briefing on it," said Tim

"I know but just say for the moment. Our Russian friends are in the shit with the Kremlin and need to redeem themselves pronto. We all know that Putin has stated that he admires Trump and the feeling seems to be reciprocated. What if Trump could get a little boost? What if our trio of scumbags were in a position to deliver it? Would that be enough of a draw to get them to come to us?"

"Of course it would, It would put them straight back on the A list of Kremlin celebrities. But how is that going to happen?"

"We are still immune from prosecution aren't we?" asked Pelham.

"We don't want to admit to further crimes and get slapped with it later," said Levy.

"For fuck's sake, get on with it, I want the Russians not you two."

"OK, I had an offer of some information that would be detrimental to Clinton. The plan was simple really. I wanted to get the access to the dirt and control when it was released. We would short key stocks and in particular the dollar."

"Short?" asked Tim.

"Sell something you don't have and hope to buy it back at a lower price, before you have to deliver it. If you sell say the dollar at, for example, one pound fifty and buy it back for one pound after you release the bad news, you would make yourself fifty percent in a few hours," said Levy.

"We have, however, been thinking. The same information that damages Clinton would help Trump. If your friends had that information, they would be in the clear and free to continue their criminal ways, with no threat from the Kremlin," said Pelham.

"What is it you exactly have?"

"We don't have anything at the present, but we know a man that does. We know some one who has a series of emails sent on an unprotected account when she was Secretary of State..."

"That is old hat. There were thousands released back in March and the FBI has dropped its investigation," interrupted Tim.

"These are new," said Pelham. Levy nodded his head in agreement.

"How new?"

"They are between Hilary and Huma Abedin."

"Who the hell is he?" asked Tim.

"You don't know much as Head of MI5, you should read more." said Levy. Tim looked annoyed so he carried on. "Huma Abedin is a her and not a he for starters. She was deputy chief of staff for Clinton up to two thousand and nine and is now the vice chair of the campaign to elect her."

"Who has these emails?"

"That is not easy to determine. They have been hacked and I have seen extracts. They are definitely authentic. There is one back in two thousand and nine which goes on about the Costa Rican president, Oscar Arias and his part in the US-backed regime change operation in Honduras."

"Don't you see the significance?" asked Pelham.

Tim did. If this was true, Clinton was guilty of a very serious breach of national security. If she made President, it could well be an impeachable offence. He also knew, that if the information was genuine and it came into MI5's possession, there was only one thing he could do. He would need, as a matter of urgency, to hand it to the FBI. The Russians may want to interfere in the US democratic process, but there was no way the UK was getting into that territory.

He had a dilemma and he was treading a very fine line. He wanted to flush out the men who had been responsible for his wife's murder, but at what cost. Revenge is a strong driving force.

"How would you proceed?"

"I think we play it as a financial matter. We have gone to them with deals in the past. We ask them to join a consortium, say they have to come up with twenty or thirty million dollars for us to gain access to the hacked emails. We cannot admit we know of their problems with the Kremlin. We only know that from MI5 and they would wonder how we knew. So, we keep that quiet and stick to the plan to short stock and currency. We let them realize the, far more, political advantage for themselves. They would do the work for us," said Pelham.

"Why would they come to the UK?"

"Because our source would be in the UK," said Levy.

"Who?" said Tim?

"MI5, or at least someone in MI5 looking to make a buck or two. You just have to get your hands on the emails?"

Chapter 15

Tim was having a bad morning. The phone had not stopped ringing since he arrived, in his office. The commute to work, from his house in Muswell Hill, had been a nightmare. As he was now head of MI5, he was a prime target for terrorists and rogue states. His home had become a fortress. He had refused to move from the semi he had shared with his wife Jackie. So the home security squad had done their best to make it secure.

The internet and the telephone had been shielded and encrypted. Security cameras were festooned like silver and black half tennis balls all over the outside of the building. He wouldn't need to have Christmas lights this year, as the entire building lit up, if even a mouse passed through the garden. There were two police on guard around the clock and everywhere he went, he had two security guards that stuck to him like shit to a blanket.

Taking public transport was off limits. So, an armoured Jaguar arrived each morning and drove him to Thames House with his bodyguards. His predecessor, Elaine Wilkins, had had much lighter security. Things had changed when she died, just months after her deputy Jeff Stills. The habit of MI5 having its key personnel dying off in quick succession was beginning to make them look a bit careless, so security was raised to a maximum.

The consequence of not being able to use public transport, slow as it was, meant that Tim had to get up at stupid o'clock and sit in the London traffic for nearly two hours in the morning and two hours in the evening. He was restricted as to what he could do from the car. Roaming networks were not secure, even with encryption, so he usually sat looking out the window grumpily at the traffic jams.

Tim was good at his administration and reading briefings. He had enough practice over the years working in embassies and briefing Ambassadors around the World, but it did not mean he enjoyed it. He had to remind himself that he had not taken the job because he wanted it. He had taken it solely with the intention of getting the Russian bastards that had caused the death of his wife Jackie. So, he got his head down and ploughed on.

Surrounded by paperwork, actually computer work, as less and less was now done on paper, he was, therefore, surprised when Harry Denham knocked and entered. They had their daily meeting schedule in about an hour's time. Feeling irritated by having his concentration interrupted he said," What's so urgent that it can't wait an hour?"

Denham ignored him, "This has just come in." He put a hand written note on Tim's desk, which had originated from the night staff officer.

Tim read. "Who is Rafiq?"

Denham settled himself into one of the chairs on the opposite side of the desk to Tim. "He is one of the agents we sent to the immigrant camp in Calais. Their brief was to keep their eyes and ears open, be on the lookout for any terrorists trying to sneak in under the radar posing as refugees."

Tim interrupted. "I didn't know we had people in the field in foreign countries."

"We don't usually, but there is such a shortage with all the threats, it became all hands to the pump. I am sure you were informed. Check you briefings." Denham could not resist having a dig at his boss.

Tim ignored the jibe. He had not been given the job because he was better qualified than Denham, but because he had the goods on the establishment, "Nizar?"

"He was in Iraq, the commander on the ground, but more importantly, he coordinates the ISIS attacks in the UK. He was linked to the underground bombers and other attempted attacks. You were involved in the death of his brother."

"Me?" Tim was surprised.

"The debacle in Wood Green, his brother was among the dead, along with some drug dealers and that Turkish agent, Yosuf"

Tim clicked. It now seemed a lifetime ago, but was in reality only a few months, when he and Yosuf had gone to Wood Green, to seek help from a Turkish drug baron. Yosuf and he had been hung out dry and were out on their own being hunted by Turkish intelligence, ISIS and MI6. The episode had culminated in a Wild West style shoot out on the streets of North London. Tim realised that one of the ISIS thugs that died. must have been this Nizar's brother. "Oh, I hadn't realised the connection."

"It is unimportant. The situation appears to be that this Nizar has had enough, a change of heart or whatever, if you chose to believe Rafiq. He wants to come home, bless his cotton socks. He wants immunity by revealing the details of a planned terrorist attack."

"What are your thoughts on it?"

"We can't plea bargain. We are not in the States. We can't technically grant him immunity from a common cold. In any event, he is a murdering piece of shit that should be hung up by his bollocks. He is British and he is a traitor. What do you expect me to say?"

Just that, what about the girl?"

"She is a kid, a stupid kid, who got herself in a stupid mess. Her sister and friend were raped and murdered, It is just sad. We can get her back through the immigration service. Pull a few strings and get her repatriated along with the other kids they are rescuing from the camp, under the Governments humanitarian programme."

"Alright, get her back to her family. One dead child is enough for any parent," said Tim.

"Her parents are Pakistani immigrants themselves. They come from one of those tribal areas. I assume they have been through quite a bit themselves before they got to the UK. At least getting their daughter back should be a little light for them," said Denham.

"Let's get Nizar back as well. Let's see if we can stop this plot. We can at least save a few British lives."

"That is a bit more of an ask. There is no way he can get through our border controls. He would be arrested by immigration immediately. We should hand him over to the French authorities. It is the only thing we can do."

"No, we get him back, even if we have to smuggle him in," said Tim.

"We can't just ignore the law. We are here to uphold it, not break it."

"We do what is best."

"Oh, and you know, what is best do you?" Denham was angry.

"Get the girl out. I will deal with Rafiq and Nizar personally."

"You expect me to stand by knowing that you are going to break the law?"

"No, I expect you to do what you have been made my deputy for. I expect you to report back everything to the Home Secretary. We both know that your primarily function here is to spy on my and report back, until they have enough to cover their own arses and they can dump me."

Denham knew that what Tim said was true, but he still was resistant to letting Tim ignore the law. "I protest..."

"Protest all you fucking want, but I am in charge here, not you. Remember that and while you remember that, you can remind your masters that unless they want to hit the headlines and spend time in the nick, they need to remember the evidence I hold on them." Tim was now angry with the hypocrisy of it.

"I don't understand?"

"You don't need to, just follow my orders."

Denham was furious and rose from the chair and made to the door. "Fuck you," he said, as he slammed the door behind him.

Tim did not know how and when, but he knew that Nizar would be useful to him in getting to the Russian bastards. He would get him back into the UK and he would stop the attack on British soil, if nothing else.

Chapter 16

Harriet Shaw, designated MI5 mole by Tim, was feeling under pressure. She had been recruited to work on cyber technology. She seriously wondered if her degree had trained her to deal with the purveyors of Hilary Clinton's private emails or, for that matter, with the person selling of them. The people most obviously interested in the emails were the Republican Party, as releasing them would damage Hilary Clinton and boost Trump. The Democrats would rather they did not surface and so had their reasons to acquire them. The Russians wanted a Trump administration and they were already focussing their cyber espionage efforts on the Democrats to dig for dirt on Clinton. Their support for Trump was based on his statements in admiration for the Russian Premier and a more isolationist foreign policy, giving the Russians more scope for a wider role globally.

"Where are the emails coming from? I thought the FBI had gone through Clinton's private server and satisfied, closed the investigation," said Harriet. She was sat in the back of black cab on the jump seat facing Mel Levy and Graham Pelham. They were heading to the Inn on the Park for their meeting with the vendor.

"Have you been following the Anthony Weiner scandal?" asked Pelham.

"Not really."

"Usual stuff, some old bloke putting it about with young women," interrupted Levy

"Quite," Pelham said, showing his disdain for the New Yorkers crass analysis. "Weiner was in the House of Representatives and got involved in what they have dubbed sexting. In brief, he allegedly sent naughty photos to several young women."

"I don't see what that has to do with Clinton?"

"Oh, the connection, he was the husband of Huma Abedin, Clinton's aid and deputy campaign manager," said Levy.

"There is an inquiry still ongoing into what they are calling Weiner gate. They have gotten hold of his electronic devices and lo and behold, more emails, with Clinton and Abedin on an unauthorised server."

"Surely these emails would be handed straight over?" asked Harriet.

"We are not buying the emails as such, we are buying the delay. Or cover story is that we want, to delay their release until after the Presidential Election on November the eighth. The assumption being, that the UK would prefer Clinton to Trump," said Pelham.

"Do we?"

"Does it matter? Tim wants us to get hold of them so he can get the Russians to the UK. Graham and I don't give a flying fuck either way. We just don't want to be banged up for the rest of our lives." Pelham nodded his agreement to Levy's statement.

"I am not very confident about this. Why me? I am not really an agent at all," said Harriet.

"Well that we can answer, it is pretty damned obvious. Whatever your boss had got going on, it has nothing to do with MI5 or National Security. It is personal. He wants these Russian bastards for one reason or another and he is not too bothered how he gets them."

Harriet sat back in the jump seat, her mind racing. They were right; she was being used by Tim. She tried to consider her options. There were none as far as she could see. Go over Tim's head to the Home Secretary, or go to Tim's deputy, Harry Denham. She instinctively knew that would not end well for her. Why had Tim chosen her for this, was the question?

"Fuck," it came to her, Tim knew. He had worked it out. When Tim was Deputy to Elaine Wilkins, she had been her eyes and ears. She had been working closely with him and reporting his every move back to her. She did not know how, but Elaine and her son had ended up dead and now Tim was running the show. He was letting her know who was boss and that he knew of her betrayal. She realised she had to get this right. Her boss was no fool.

The cab pulled up at the hotel opposite Hyde Park and they were soon sat in one of the luxurious rooms. Pelham started the conversation. "Mr Levy and I are only acting as brokers in this matter. This young lady, who wants to remain nameless, represents one of the UK's security services. We understand that you have certain email transcripts. We further understand that these may be available for purchase."

The woman sat opposite was in her fifties. She was clearly some sort of court official. She had seen an opportunity to get rich and she wanted it. This was her chance to be a somebody and she knew the window of opportunity was small. The email transcripts would be released to the FBI in a week at most. She needed to cash in now. The approach by Levy had been a Godsend. She knew that both the Republicans and the Democrats wanted the emails, but feared the consequences of exposure in the US. Levy had paid for her to fly first class to London, stay at this beautiful hotel and fly back tomorrow. She had this one chance to get rich and change her life.

She spoke, "Twenty million dollars." She had no idea what they were worth, but she thought that the outcome of a Presidential

Election must be worth a lot. If she had more intellect and better contacts, she could have received fifty, but she was what she was and where she was.

"One million," said Pelham.

She shook her head. "They are worth a lot more," Levy and Pelham knew that. They also knew that they were the ones paying for them. Tim had made it perfectly clear, that if they wanted to escape prosecution in the States and in the UK, they had better put up the money.

Harriet found her voice." Enough, five million, take it or I walk."

Levy and Pelham had the look on their faces of someone who had just bitten into a Lemon. They knew that they could have beaten the price lower and were annoyed to see their illicit gains being squandered so casually. Harriet, on the other hand knew that she had to get the transcripts for Tim and she certainly did not give a jot for the two crook's bank balances.

After a pause and seeing the look of determination in Harriet's eyes, they agreed.

"Do it," Harriet looked at Levy.

The laptop was brought out and five million dollars moved from Levy's account to an offshore account. He wrote on a piece of paper and handed it to the woman, "The transcripts." She handed him the SD card. "The money is in this account and the code allows you to access it and do what you want with it. The account is untraceable." One thing Levy was good at was hiding money and money laundering. In fact, he was the master.

The card was inserted in the port of the laptop and the emails verified. They left and were soon in a cab back to Thames House. It was now up to Harriet to get the Russians to bite.

Chapter 17

Nizar and Aleena spent a quiet night in a Premier Inn on the outskirts of Calais. It was not the most luxurious of accommodation, but it was a step up from an abandoned farmhouse. Nizar had contemplated making a break for it during the night. He knew Aleena would be alright as a minor and would be repatriated. He, on the other hand, was facing an uncertain future.

On his own, sought by ISIS and every counter terrorist organisation in Europe, he realised he had little chance of making it. All in all, his only realistic chance of survival was through Rafiq. He had to hope he could cut some sort of deal with MI5, if and when, they got him to the UK. The plot in the UK was the only strong card in his hand and he was determined to play it to the full.

They sat in the dinning room, eating the serve yourself breakfast. It was a cold offering, but the coffee and croissants were good. Rafiq sat opposite them and seemed to be enjoying the food at least. He had spent the last month in the Jungle in Calais and he was also happy at his change in circumstances. A bed and even a cold breakfast was a definite improvement on conditions in the camp.

"Well?" said Nizar.

Rafiq thought for a while before responding. He had nothing but loathing for the man sat opposite him. Here was a man who had been involved in some of the worst atrocities in modern times and he, Rafiq, was set to help him possibly escape any form of justice.

Nizar had participated in murders, beheadings and rape. Now, he was looking to get away with it. Rafiq regretted not pulling the trigger the previous evening.

"I have my instructions. You will get back to the UK, but beyond that, I know nothing. Just get your stuff together and we shall be on our way."

Rafiq had not been idle and the rental a car was delivered to the hotel. Nizar and Aleena were surprised when they emerged from the lobby to see Rafiq at the wheel of the Twingo. "Don't look so surprised. I am not on the run. I have a perfectly good credit card and driver's license. Get in and we can be off."

The drive into Calais was difficult and slow. The French police were out in force, ensuring the orderly clearing of the camp. The migrants were being systematically rounded up, registered and bussed to diverse locations in France for housing. The roads were cordoned off by the police to minimise the risk of the vast number of, in the main, young men causing disruption and disorder. There had been rioting in the period leading up to the clearing of the Jungle and the authorities were ensuring there would be no repetition.

Coaches were lined up at the various collection and processing points. Queues were organised and supervised. A quiet calm had taken hold. The camp was being systematically erased. Bulldozers were pushing the poorly constructed buildings down. Trucks were being loaded with rubbish and rubble and trucking it away.

Many of the former residents of the Jungle had resigned themselves to the situation. Most had made their way to Calais in the hope of, somehow, getting to Britain. They had walked the railway tracks through the Tunnel that took the trains under the North Sea from Calais to Dover. Some had been killed in their attempts. They had hidden in the backs of trucks bound for the ferry crossing. They had tried clinging to the axels of the articulated trucks queuing to board the ferry. Some had made it, most were caught and returned to France and others had died.

Rafiq was stopped as he approached the bus station. He had a brief conversation with a police officer, who departed to consult with a superior. "You two should say nothing and stay quiet," said Rafiq. He had noticed that Nizar, suspecting Rafiq might hand him to the French authorities, was becoming agitated. Turning his head to address him, he said, "Look if I was going to hand you in, I could just have got the police to nab you at the hotel if I wanted to, so just stay calm."

The officer returned. Phone calls had been made and the situation verified. The policemen directed Rafiq to a holding area were a group of young men were gathered. "Stay in the car," he said to Nizar "Aleena, come with me. Say goodbye, to each other."

Aleena looked confused and unsure. She was reluctant to leave Nizar. "Listen," continued Rafiq. "The British have taken in a number of minors, refugees under eighteens as part of their humanitarian relief policy. This group here are those selected to be re-homed in the UK. Your name, Aleena, is on the list. You will be taken to a centre in Kent, given medical treatment and reunited with you parents."

She hesitated for a moment. Then she threw her arms around Nizar and having given him a big hug, she stepped from the car. "You have to understand that your friend, your sister and your departure from the conflict was front page news. If we put you on a plane back to the UK, the press would be all over it. This is the only way we could get you back quietly. It will not last of course, but at least it gives all concerned a chance to prepare for the deluge of press interest. OK?"

She nodded and half managed a smile. Rafiq walked her over to the UK Immigration officer who was attempting to avoid chaos and load the coach with a random assortment of young migrants. It was self evident that a number of the so-called children waiting to be boarded were in their twenties and even thirties. The Officer in charge was fully aware of that fact, but it was of no concern. The admitting of these so-called minors was a public relations exercise by the Government, designed to let the World know that it was doing its fair share in the crises. Without passports, papers or any sort ID, it was impossible to realistically determine the age of those being taken into care in the UK.

Initially the Government had bussed the children in coaches and the press had been able to take pictures of those on board through the windows. Now, the windows had been white washed to obscure the occupants and avoid scrutiny. The first busloads had raised public outcry, as it was clear that many of the so-called rescued children had beards and looked much older than eighteen.

Rafiq watched as Aleena got on a coach. She gave him a smile, surpassed a tear and waived. It was not ideal, but at least it bought time. The alternative scenario was to have had her arrested by the French Police with the use of an international arrest warrant. She would have then been deported to the UK to face terrorism charges. She would be collected from the Reception Centre and in the care of Social Services, she would be taken to hospital.

Rafiq returned to the car. "It appears that we are to go the seaside." He started the engine and began to drive south along the coast road. The charity worker helping to load the busses dialled a number on her mobile phone and the voice at the other end congratulated her on her observational skills.

Chapter 18

Yerik Nikhil and Lesta were fully aware that they were not flavour of the month with the Kremlin. Each of them had been experiencing minor setbacks in their lives on a daily basis. Parking tickets, permissions denied and health and safety fines were a constant reminder that they were out of favour.

They were attending a meeting of the Baltic Bank holding company, their highly successful money-laundering vehicle. They had rented an office for the occasion in St Petersburg, rather than meet at the Company's headquarters in Moscow, in the vain hope of obtaining some relief from the constant surveillance they were all under by the State Security Service.

The Security Service was not baulked so easily and they all arrived with their obligatory surveillance followers in support. They had not intentionally set out to upset the Kremlin, but had succeeded, big time, without realising it. It had all started when they had been offered some anti aircraft missiles. The missiles in question were BuKs and were of the mobile variety, that meant they could be deployed quickly, fired and moved to another location. They were the type of missile that had been deployed in the Ukraine and had been used to shoot down a passenger jet in error.

They had been offered the missiles by a fellow Russian arms dealer and they had found ready buyers for them in the form of ISIS. In good faith, they had bought them and arranged their onward sale to the extremists in Syria at a vast profit.

That is when it went tits up for the three Russians. Firstly, it turned out that the missiles were not the same type of missile that had been used to down the passenger jet, they were the actual ones. It transpired that the seller had been commissioned to quietly scrap the launchers and so, dispose of the evidence and the link to the Russian State. In fact, he had pocketed a tidy sum for the service. Greed had, however, got the better of him and seeing a chance to make even more money, they sold the BuKs onto the three.

Yerik, Nikhil and Lesta thought they had made a quick buck when they found a dealer who would sell them to ISIS in Syria. Things had not gone according to plan. The Kremlin found out that the missile batteries had not been destroyed, which caused a certain amount of annoyance and naturally, the death of the individual that had sold them on, instead of destroying them quietly. Further annoyance, this time aimed at Yerik, Nikhil and Lesta, was generated when it was discovered that they were selling them to the very people Russian jets were bombing in Syria. The idea that ISIS would be using a Russian missile system to shoot down Russian plans was never going to be popular in the Kremlin.

The three were forced to tell the Russian air force when and where the BuKs were to be delivered to ISIS. The convoy containing the missiles was targeted and destroyed by a Russian air strike. They, obviously, did not receive payment from ISIS as the missiles were no more and the Kremlin was not impressed with the whole affair.

The three sat round the table. "I am guessing we are all feeling the heat?" said Lesta.

"What do you fucking think? Of course we are," said Yerik. "The question is, how do we get out of this pile of shit?"

"There is no point in wrangling among ourselves, so calm down and listen. I have had contact with Mel Levy and he may have a solution to our problem. He may not know he has the solution, as he does not know the problem, but he may inadvertently come up with a way out for us. If it is what I think it is, we will be back in everyone's good books in no time," said Nikhil.

"What do you want, a round of applause? Just tell us what he said."

"He and Pelham have been working on a scheme to get us an edge in the currency market. The idea is, that if Trump gets elected president of the US, confidence will fall and the dollar will drop in value. He is suggesting we short the dollar and cash in when it happens."

"Well that is fucking obvious, except that Clinton is odds on to be elected. So it's bollocks."

"Just shut up and listen for a minute. Pelham is saying that they have a contact who has something on Clinton, that is a game changer," said Nikhil.

"She seems pretty bullet proof. They have thrown enough mud at her to take any normal candidate out of the running, but as they are both so unpopular, she seems to be the best of the crop. So what does our friend think could sway public opinion against her?" said Lesta,

"He has someone in MI5 who wants to bump up their retirement fund."

"You are fucking kidding me. You are suggesting we do business with MI5. No way, it has to be a set up," said Lesta.

"Not MI5, a rogue employee. Pelham has the in. We just need to meet, assess the quality of the information, buy it and hand it to the Kremlin. We all know that the Kremlin is doing everything it can to get Trump in power. He is a lot less hard-line to us than Clinton. They have been hacking away, looking for dirt on her and we can just hand it to them on a plate. It will get us off the hook and everybody live happilly ever after."

"Say we buy the idea that this MI5 person has something and is willing to trade. Do we have a plan?" asked Yerik.

"We stick to Levy and Pelham's idea. We are in it for the money. We are just looking for a bit of inside information that will allow us to gain an edge in the currency market and make a few roubles. It is a fine line, but insider trading is better than aiding a foreign power, especially if MI5 is your boss."

There was silence as the three men considered the matter. In reality, there was not much of a decision. None of them had anything else on the table. There was no doubting that, getting Trump elected, would make them the flavour of the month at the Kremlin.

"What's next?"

"We have to go to London and meet," said Nikhil.

"Why would we do that?" said Yerik

"Good faith apparently, assurances that we are not connected to some Soviet plot. In essence, it is to solve the conscience of the person at MI5. It allows them to lie to themselves that this just a business transaction. That is what Levy has told me. I don't believe him. I also think that whoever is selling, knows of Levy, his criminal past for dodgy dealing and doesn't trust him. They want to deal direct and make sure; they are not short changed along the way."

"The latter makes more sense."

"The question is: do we go?"

"What choice do we have? Stay here and wait for the Kremlin to get tired of us?"

Chapter 19

Tim and his three agents walked into the takeaway kebab shop in Wood Green. The shop assistant immediately reached below the counter and pressed a button that alerted those upstairs of their arrival. One of the agents closed the glass door and turned the sign hanging from it from "open" to "closed."

As soon as the car Tim had arrived in turned into the high street, his memories came flooding back. This was where his life had changed forever. Just a few months ago he had arrived here with Yosuf, hunted by ISIS, the Turks and MI6, now he was back, as head of MI5. As he looked at the corner of the street, he realised that this was the exact spot where Yosuf had died. Now he knew it was also the spot where Nizar's brother had died. He had been one of the hit squad, sent by ISIS, to kill him.

It was difficult to comprehend that an unremarkable street, in a suburb of North London could be the catalyst for so much change in his life. The death of Nizar's brother had set in motion a chain of events that, ultimately, led to the death of Tim's wife. The memories hung heavily on him, as he stood in the takeaway.

"Tell Mo that we are MI5 and I wish to speak to him. This is not a raid. I merely want to talk," said Tim to the startled assistant. He stood aside as the assistant walked past him and the end of the counter to the heavy reinforced steel door at the bottom of the stairs at the rear.

The assistant spoke and Tim showed his face to the camera

positioned next to the intercom. "I know you," the voice said.

"Yes, you do. Things have changed since the last time I was here. Just unlock the door. I just want a conversation with you." Tim waited and clearly, there was some hesitation and reluctance on behalf of the occupants to admit him.

"Don't fuck about, "said Tim. "My gang is a lot bigger than yours."

The door clicked, Tim entered and climbed the stairs. He entered the room he and Yosuf had been in those few months earlier. Since then, Tim had run a check on the owner. He now knew his real name, Mo Misare and the extent of his suspected heroin importation activities.

There were seven gang members sat at tables looking at him as he entered. All activity had stopped. Coffee and backgammon sat unattended as Mo's men turned their attention to Tim.

"I cannot say I am pleased to see you," said Mo.

"I didn't expect a warm welcome, but I need you to help me with a small problem."

"That makes me even less pleased. The last time I helped you and your friend, my shop was blown up and three of my men died."

"I fully understand, but you don't really have a choice do you? You may be able to get away with your drug activities, to an extent with the police, but if I decide you are of interest to MI5, you will be banged up before the end of the day. Trust me."

Mo just nodded." What do you want of me?"

"I want you to do what you do best, smuggling. I need some people brought in from France. Are you still using the route which Yosuf and I used?"

"How do I know you are not tricking me? I give you my

importation method and then you just inform the coast guard."

"Stop fucking about, you have ten seconds to decide to help, or the lot of you will be dragged out of here under the terrorist laws. Don't forget you are not a UK or EU citizen. You will be deported back to Turkey and barred from the UK. I will make it my mission to make sure of it. The other drug gangs would take your place before tea time."

"How many people?" Mo resigned himself to the reality of the situation.

"Two," said Tim.

Chapter 20

Jimmy Buari woke with a sense of anticipation. It was early and the sun had not yet broken cover. He could hear Sinita breathing deeply next to him as she slept. She stirred slightly and rolled over as he got from the bed, walked out of the room and made his way to the bathroom.

He had still not had the call from Nizar confirming the target, but today he would be one-step closer to fulfilling his destiny. He relived his bladder and stepped under the shower that dribbled tepid water into the bath. He pulled the shower curtain round and began to wash. Having showered, he returned to the bedroom and dressed quietly in the semi darkness. He managed to complete the process without waking Sinita. He did not want to talk. He was too tense. He knew today and what he had to accomplish was dangerous. If he were stopped, all the planning would have been for nothing.

He made his way from the flat down the street, to where the car was parked. The sun was just starting to rise on what would be a mild, dry and sunny day as he started the engine. Even at this early hour, the traffic was beginning to build for the morning rush to work.

The Toll crossing on the M25 was causing the usual back up to the traffic in Dartford and he found the slow moving procession of vehicles trying to get to the motorway frustrating. His nerves were on edge, but he knew he had to remain calm and not get into an altercation with another driver. The last thing he wanted to do was draw attention to himself.

Jimmy finally turned onto the motorway and made his slow progress over the Queen Elizabeth II Bridge. The toll booths had been replaced by an online payment system. He had made sure the previous evening that he had sufficient credit on his account to cover his trip over the Bridge.

Once over the River, he made fast progress and turned off, headed to Southend. The traffic was hardly moving in the other direction, but as he was heading away from London, he encountered little resistance to his progress. He missed the turn off for Pitsea and ended up driving round Basildon before he located the industrial estate he was looking for.

Jimmy had the padlock key he had collected from the dead drop in the Great Wood and he had memorised the entry code. All he needed to do was locate the storage unit on the industrial estate.

He followed the signs to the industrial Estate. There were a collection of small workshops containing various businesses, from tyre fitters to cardboard box suppliers. He could see the large red box on the top of the building he was looking for. He parked out front, away from the CCTV covering the immediate area and pulled his hoody up to cover his face as he exited the car and approached the storage facility.

Jimmy located the key pad and entered the small side door. There was a larger roller door that opened with the same code, that allowed bigger items to be taken in and out. The unit Jimmy was looking for was far smaller and he soon got the hang of the numbering system employed and located it. The door was padlocked and he used the Key, that had been in the envelope to unlock the door.

The room was totally empty apart from a holdall positioned in the centre. He walked in and retrieved it. His heart was beating so fast he felt giddy as he bent to pick it up. His hands trembled as he pulled back the zipper on the bag. He took a deep breath to calm himself before pulling back the opening to reveal the contents

His hands were trembling as he realised that this was really it. The moment he had planned for, for so long. There, in the bag was the bomb. It has been made by another group of ISIS supporters. People he would never know, or ever meet. They, in turn, had never met the people who had acquired and supplied them with the bomb making material. Isolated, but united in a common cause they had worked together to bring it to fruition.

Jimmy now was the last link in the chain, a very long chain that stretched across seas and continents to the fighters in Syria, Iraq and the Yemen. Separated by distance, but brought close by belief and faith, they all contracted to the ideal of the reestablishment of the Caliphate and the destruction of non-believers. It was now all down to Jimmy to bring terror into the heart of London.

He examined the bomb. It was a pipe bomb. The casing and it contents would blast shrapnel in a wide arc, maiming and killing those within its range. A phone was the means of detonation. Dial the number and the detonator would respond. The battery and sim had been removed from the phone to avoid any mishap. He knew he had to ensure the battery was fully charged and then insert both sim and battery into the phone to enable the device.

As he drove away, he was eager to get started. He had just over three weeks to wait. All he needed was a call from Nizar, confirming the target and giving the go ahead. He, Jimmy Buari, would fulfil his destiny and strike a blow for the cause of Islam.

Chapter 21

The Twingo was far from luxurious. Rafiq was driving and Nizar was wedged in the passenger seat alongside. Neither were small men and it felt claustrophobic in the small runabout. Matters were hardly aided by the fact that they could not be described as friends travelling together. Nizar was fully aware that Rafiq considered him a traitor and given the option, would happily put a bullet in him before dumping him along the side of the N road they were now following south.

Nizar had initially attempted conversation, but Rafiq had made it plain that he had no intention of easing the tension between them by indulging in any form of small talk. Having dropped Aleena at the transit point in Calais, they had eventually escaped the series of major roads leading to and from the town and made their way onto the series of minor roads that would take them further.

Nizar could not help thinking of Aleena. They had both shared the dream of a pure Islamic state, uncorrupted by Western ideas and laws, a place where they could live and die as pure Muslims. Now it looked as if the dream was receding. In Syria, the Russians had seized the stage and Aleppo would fall to the combined forces of Assad's Government and the Russians. ISIS was becoming isolated and the route between its forces in Iraq and Syria was blocked by opposition forces.

In Iraq, it was only a matter of time it seemed, that the combined force of Kurds and Iraqis would gain control and then the Caliphate would be consigned to history yet again.

Nizar knew that he had given all that he had to the dream and it had broken him. There was only so much a man could bear, only so much killing and only so much loss. He was no longer a part of anything. His brother was dead. He was hunted as a terrorist. He was no longer the brave fighter he had burnt out and now just wanted go home.

The weather was very mild, the trees lining the long straight road were coppery red where the leaves still lingered, waiting for winter to commence. The countryside in Northern France reminded him of England. It was green. Iraq had been grey. He had been brought up with green and moved to grey. In a small part of his heart, he had longed for the return to green. When he had travelled to Syria to train, he had hoped to spread the green into that part of the world, to recreate the land of gardens of paradise. They had not created paradise. They had added further death and destruction to a land already broken in the aftermath of the invasion by America and its allies.

At least Aleena would be back with her parents soon. He had at least secured that much. She would not be charged and would be allowed to go home. It was part of the deal he had made. He knew he had but one chip to play his hand with. Jimmy Buari was that chip. He would trade him for a new identity and a new life.

Rafiq tensed in the driver's seat. He kept looking in the rear view mirror and grasped the wheel more firmly. His foot pressed down harder on the accelerator pedal. The car gradually responded to the increase in fuel flowing to the engine, but it was never designed for power and the increase in speed was less than spectacular.

Rafiq was now looking more into the rear view mirror than he was the road ahead. Nizar sank lower into his seat in order to look in the passenger side mirror. He caught a glimpse of what had grabbed Rafiq's attention. The silver Blue BMW filled the rear view mirror. Nizar managed to turn his body inwards and pushing against Rafiq in the confined space, craned his neck to look from the rear window of the Twingo.

It did not take a genius to come to the conclusion, that they were being chased by two men in the car behind. He had no way of knowing, that they had been tailed at a discreet distance since Calais. Nizar was on the ISIS wanted list and they were not going to give up easily. Adnan may have been dealt with, but he had not been alone. Sympathisers were all over. They knew that Aleena and he were in Calais. Adnan would have been reporting back. When Rafiq and he had dropped her off, they had been spotted and a phone call made alerting their pursuers.

The road was deserted, save for the Twingo and the BMW. These roads, that once saw heavy traffic in the summer as the annual progress of holiday makers made their way to the south of France and the sun, were no longer much used. Countless bars and bed and breakfast businessess had closed along these routes as the motorway system expanded. Only local traffic really made use of the lesser roads.

Rafiq looked across at Nizar, there was fear in his eyes. The car they were in was no match for the pursuing vehicle, there was no possibility of help. "The gun," said Nizar.

"In my left hand coat pocket."

There was no way that he could reach the gun. He would need to somehow reach over the centre consul,across Rafiq's lap and then have arms long enough to get to the coat pocket that was pressed against the driver's door. He had to try though. He undid the safety belt and tried to wriggle into the rear of the car. He hoped to be able to reach Rafiq's left side from the back seat somehow.

He did not get the opportunity. The BMW rammed the rear of their car. There was a grinding of metal and the Twingo rocked side to side. Rafiq manage to maintain control and carry on. They both knew that it was only a matter of time, before the far heavier car chasing them, ran them off the road into the row of trees that lined it.

Nizar was half way into the rear. He had managed to turn himself and was on his knees facing the back of the car when he was thrown across Rafiq's lap. For a split second, it seemed as though the car would roll over, but it made the sharp right turn onto the dirt track.

Rafiq had spotted the track running off, almost at right angles to the road and had slewed the wheel and miraculously, managed to keep the car upright as it made the turn. The BMW had been caught unprepared and had continued on past the turning. Rafiq had bought them a little distance and a little time, as the BMW came to stop and did a three point turn to resume the chase.

The track was edged by bushes and trees, obviously planted as a windbreak by the landowner. Further along would be a barn or a farmhouse, probably no longer in use. Stacked high off the track were the round bales of hay, covered in tarpaulins, winter feed for the livestock. Pulling the wheel once again to the right, Rafiq headed across the bumpy ground to the nearest stack of hay bales. He drove around them and parked, facing at right angles to the track. The BMW was only seconds away and would soon come into view. "Get out," said Rafiq.

They were at the top of a slope above the track. The BMW would pass below them. Rafiq drew the gun from his pocket. "Push the car into the track," he screamed

Nizar ran behind the car and pushed for all he was worth. He could hear the sound of the BMW getting closer and louder. He pushed harder and the Twingo gathered speed as it rolled towards the track. From his crouched position behind the car, Nizar saw the BMW race into view. For a brief second he feared that it would speed past before he could push the Twingo into its path.

The next seconds became a blur. The BMW came into view and was immediately confronted with the Twingo blocking its path. The driver pulled at the wheel violently and nearly avoided the car in front of it. The manoeuvre was only partly successful and it struck the Twingo a glancing blow before it cannoned off the track and came to sudden halt in the drainage ditch that bordered the track. The rear of the Twingo spun and Nizar was thrown to the ground. He was aware of Rafiq rushing past him towards the bogged down BMW, gun in hand.

The passenger of the BMW had struck the windscreen, blood ran down his face blinding him. Rafiq fired three times and hit him twice. The blood running down his face was joined by a fountain of blood that spurted from the artery in his neck severed by one of the bullets.

Nizar got to his feet as Rafiq rounded the car to the driver's side now furthest away, following the three sixty degree spin. He saw Rafiq raise his gun and fire through the window. Then he saw the muzzle flash and the interior of the BMW light up as the driver returned fire.

Rafiq had a look of stunned surprise on his face as the red stain spread across his chest. He fired into the car one more time and then sank slowly down into the mud. He dropped the gun and moved his hands to his chest. In almost slow motion, Nizar saw the life force drain from him. He fell forward. All was suddenly still.

Nizar dragged himself to his feet and slowly made his way towards the BMW. He crouched low as he approached, avoiding the possibility of the driver seeing him in the rear view mirror. He held his breath as he crept alongside the car. His target was the gun lying beside Rafiq that had fallen from his hand as he died.

He reached the gun and griping it, jumped to his feet, aiming it at the cars interior. He need not have worried. Rafiq's second shot had found it's mark. The driver lay slumped over the wheel, the side of his head missing, brains and blood sprayed across the dash and passenger seat.

Nizar stood breathing slowly, letting the adrenaline rush subside. Calming himself, he began the clear up. He needed time. It took him nearly and hour to drag the bodies into the Twingo and clean the mess from the inside the BMW. It was not perfect, but at least from the outside, there was no evidence of blood and brains dripping down the windows and roof of the interior. It would have to do. He drove the Twingo containing the dead and parked it behind the hay bales. He hoped, that they would not be found before he was way well on his way.

Getting the BMW back onto the track proved difficult. Every time he tried to drive, it became bogged in the mud alongside the track. The wheels spun, throwing up dirt as they did so. The hay bales proved, once again, to be his salvation, as he gathered large clumps of the dried grass and piled them under the wheels of the car. Eventually, he had the car pointing back towards the highway. He drove slowly along the track, careful not to get bogged down again.

In his pocket, he had Rafiq's phone. He knew that Rafiq had been expecting a call from MI5, to tell him where to rendezvous, so they could bring him to England. Nizar would answer that call, hope that they would believe that he had no hand in their agent's death and still get him home.

Chapter 22

Aleena was sat up in bed in Maidstone Hospital in Kent. She had been exhausted when she arrived the previous day. The journey from the Jungle on the coach, had been less than pleasant, but was far better than the experiences she had had the last few months. She had been woken early and breakfast had been served at around eight o'clock. Now, she had to sit and wait for the doctors to do their rounds.

Sitting in the hospital bed left her reflecting on the last few weeks of her life. It had all seemed so exciting and wonderful when she, Mariam and Haniya had set out for Turkey. Now her sister and her friend were dead. It was not meant to be this way. They were supposed to be living in a land of paradise. They were to be the brides of the brave warriors, that would build a new Islamic State.

They, she, her sister and friend had communicated with the women of ISIS on-line. They had been told how glorious and honourable their lives would be. They had been told how they were would be building a new, pure Islam. They had been told of the corrupting influence of the West. They had been shown how the Imperialists were killing their brothers around the World. They had believed.

She now knew that war was not glorious. War attracted the good and the righteous, but it also attracted the fanatics, the misfits, the rapists, the child molesters and sociopaths. War not only brought out the best of mankind, but also the worst. She had learned that devoted believers of any faith could and would use their beliefs to justify their own corruption. She had seen how the establishment of a true Islamic state had been usurped and used to justify mans basic instincts.

She had seen men and women being beheaded for no more than having a cell phone. She had seen pregnant women raped. She had seen her sister and friend raped and murdered. She had been used.

The door opened and a doctor entered. "How do you feel?"

"I am ok."

"That is good, but there are a few things we need to discuss." He sat on the edge of the bed and referred to the file he was holding. "Some are minor issues we can deal with by medicating, others we need to examine a little more closely. Do you understand?"

She nodded her head and looked out of the window into the middle distance. She was not sure she wanted to know what had happened to her body. She felt detached by listening and acknowledging, it would make it all a reality. She was so much wiser now than that schoolgirl she had been in Walsall, looking at the Jihadi cause on the internet. Dreams and anticipation had been replaced by harsh reality, a reality that the doctor would now, inadvertently, make her confront. She would prefer to just let it be forgotten, but that could not be.

"You have an STD, well several in fact."

She was naive. Her parents were strict and her knowledge of sex was limited. She had been raped repeatedly, but she knew little of the world. She was, after all, only a fourteen-year-old child. "I don't understand," she said simply.

The doctor, a young man himself, of Pakistan descent, was finding it difficult to deal with the young girl in front of him. He saw himself as a devote Muslim, but was planets apart from the girl before him. Their life experiences were separated by a gulf that he

99

found hard to reconcile. His medical interpretation of the patient before him was that of extreme child abuse. It was hard to recognise that this had been carried out by his brother Muslims, whose radical beliefs overrode any sense of humanity.

"Some diseases, viruses and bacterium are transferred from one person to another during the act of sexual intercourse," he said awkwardly. There was a silence. She concentrated on the view from the window.

He continued. "We can treat the syphilis with antibiotics."

He waited to see if she would ask any further questions. She continued to look away.

"There are a number of other issues. You will need surgery to deal with the prolapsed anus and vagina. A specialist surgeon will come and see you and tell you all about the procedure. Is that OK?"

Aleena just nodded her head and a tear ran down her cheek.

"There is a further issue and I have arranged for a counsellor to speak to you when I have finished explaining"

"I don't want my parents to know. I have shamed my father and my family. Do they know I am here?"

The doctor looked to the nurse who shook her head. "They haven't been informed yet. You can discuss that and other matters with the counsellor."

"I just can't face them at the moment," the tears were running down her cheeks.

""It will be alright. Let's leave this for now. We can discuss it all later. I will get you started on the antibiotics and then we can talk further."

The nurse signalled to the counsellor, who had arrived during the consultation and was waiting by the door. The doctor, seeing her said." This is Mariam Mir the counsellor. She will talk things through with you and she can access the various support, that is out there to help you readjust and cope."

On hearing the name, Mariam, Aleena broke down completely and curling up into a ball began to sob.

His training had never prepared him for this. He had often to deliver grave news, but never had he seen such a dreadful and truly sorrowful situation. Words failed him and he left the bedside. He gestured to Mariam to follow him into the corridor out of earshot.

"I have explained a number of issues, but I just could bring myself to tell her that she will be unlikely to have children."

The social worker nodded understandingly. "It is difficult. I will work with psychologist and see how the matter is best broached."

"There is something more. She is HIV positive. She will be on a lifetime of medication I am afraid, a constant reminder of events to her".

"Not only her, her family," said Mariam.

Chapter 23

A J Chauffer Cars Limited, the sign proclaimed above the garage in Knightsbridge. The premises were a luxury car showroom, exhibiting the best of the best in car bling. Tim could hardly fail to be impressed with the line up of Ferraris, Lamborghinis and other exotic super cars as he entered. As was now the norm, he was accompanied by his ever-present bodyguards. The actual chauffer limo service was a subsidiary part of the dealership business and did not have a separate office. Most of the bookings for the service were by email or telephone and there was no need for a physical presence. The hire fleet was housed and maintained in the workshops, where the drivers would collect the vehicle ordered and then drive to the client.

"How may I help you gentleman," asked the well manicured and bespoke suited sales assistant as they entered.

"I should like to speak to AJ. I phoned ahead. My name is Anthony Burr."

"I'll see if he is available, please wait," the assistant disappeared into the office area off to the left side of the showroom. Tim's entourage began to examine the cars, opening doors and sitting in them.

After a short wait, a balding middle-aged man, dressed in a sports jacket appeared from the office area. He was dark skinned and obviously of Middle Eastern heritage. The majority of the wealth and the market for these types of vehicles were with the sons of the oil rich sheiks. They could be seen driving their super cars all around the area, sowing their wild oats before taking up their roles as respected leaders of their various dominions.

"Mr Burr?" AJ extended his hand, "call me AJ."

Tim shook his hand. AJ had the natural inbuilt charm of a salesman. "May we go somewhere private?"

AJ led them to a meeting room among the office area. The two bodyguards waited outside as Tim and AJ entered. The room had a central table with six chairs, the walls were lined with paintings and photos of cars and car related activities. AJ took little notice of Tim's disciples. He was used to his wealthy clients and their personal security.

They sat and Tim declined coffee. AJ spoke first. "I don't believe we have met. I tend to know every serious car collector. It is small world in the exotic car market."

"I am not in the market to buy. I wish to hire a car from you."

AJ looked disappointed. He did not really want to waste his time on somebody who had less than a quarter of a million pounds, "I will get a colleague to organise matters," he said, dismissing Tim as a time waster.

"Please sit down, I haven't finished what I was saying." AJ was slightly taken aback by the blunt order, but he sat. He started to protest. "Just be quiet," said Tim, removing his id from his inside coat pocket and placing it on the table. AJ retrieved and read it. He remained quiet, Tim had his full attention.

"I require the hire of a limo, armoured of course, for a week or so. I need you to provide the vehicle, as the people who will be using it have used your services in the past. Using your services will avoid any chance of them being suspicious. You will treat the transaction in the normal way, same booking procedure, same methods of

103

payment and the same service. Do you understand?"

"I understand but ...."

Tim interrupted, "There will be a few differences, Firstly the car should be delivered to us for a few hours, where we shall make a few modifications."

"You are going to bug it?"

"And link it to a tracking system. There will be one further difference, the driver will be ours."

"I am only too happy to co-operate."

"Of course you are." Tim produced an envelope and removed the contents. He slid the paperwork across the table to AJ. "You will sign this."

AJ looked down at the documentation, "The official Secrets Act?"

"It is a matter of national Security, so you are being informed that you are subject to the provisions of the Act. Should you breach it, you may be subject to imprisonment. Sign the form there, to acknowledge receiving it and that you understand. " AJ signed. "Thank you."

Time rose and they shook hands. "Thank you for your co-operation. The tech guys will be over to sort the car."

Tim returned to the Jaguar parked on the forecourt followed by his guards. They took a last wistful glance at the Ferraris and drove north out of the centre of London. An hour later and they entered the drive of a large mansion in Bishops Drive, known as millionaire's row locally. The houses were a stones throw from Kenwood House and Gardens.

The agent from Golding Gilchrest was already there waiting on them. He greeted Tim as he exited the car. "Welcome," he said shaking Tim's hand with gusto. It was clear from his facial expression that he was less than impressed with the new potential purchaser standing before him. Tim did not look like the normal billionaire client who could afford to buy this property.

Tim gave the agent no time to consider matters "Show me round." Any hesitation the agent may wish to exhibit as to Tim's credentials were quickly dispelled, as he was flanked by the two agents.

The property was palatial, eight bedrooms, countless bathrooms and servants quarters. Outside there was a pool and spa complex, formal garden and a tennis court. It had it all, including the cinema complex. Tim thought that he would not mind living here himself.

"I realise the décor may not be to everyone's taste, but I am sure Sir could make it his own with a good interior designer," the Agent was twittering on in the background as Tim continued his inspection.

The house was fully furnished. The owner, it transpired, was hoping to negotiate not only the sale of the property, but also its contents. It was ready to be moved into. It was what Tim needed.

They entered the vast dining room with a table big enough for the Lord Major's banquet. "Sit down and be quiet," said Tim, who with the effervescing AJ, was reaching his limit of patience with salesmen for the day.

The agent looked slightly surprised, but being used to the vagaries of the super rich sat and shut up. "Thank you," continued Tim. "I don't want to buy it. I just want to borrow it for a few weeks."

"That's not possible. The owner is clear in his intention to sell. He has just acquired a much larger property further along the Avenue. I assure you that he would not consider a rental."

"I didn't say rent. I said borrow. Now I understand the actual owner is in residence just a few doors away. Give him a bell and say we are popping in to see him. There's a good chap."

"I Don't know who you think you are, but I want you to leave now." The young man was angry and tried to rise to his feet. One of Tim's bodyguards immediately pushed him back into his seat.

"Please do not make sudden threatening moves," he said firmly. The colour drained from the agents face.

Tim waived the bodyguard away. "Sorry about that, they are there to protect me and tend to shoot first and ask questions later. Now please listen to me and no more nonsense."

Tim explained that MI5 would like the use the property for security reasons and the young man agreed to make the necessary introduction to the owner. They all then moved five doors down Bishops Avenue and met with the owner.

The Estate Agent waited with one of the bodyguards while Tim, his remaining guard and the owner sat down in another room.

"Thank you for seeing me," said Tim.

"Always glad to help the security forces," he replied in a New York accent.

"I would greatly appreciate it if you would lend us your very nice house for a couple of weeks for some visiting guests," said Tim.

"That does seem a bit of a big request and I should say, I am reluctant to do so."

"I did anticipate that, but I do feel that you would be persuaded"

"How's that?"

"Would you mind phoning this number in the US, it is mid morning there and you will be put straight through, I assure you?"

Tim handed him a card with the number on.

"CIA, Deputy Director," he read the card aloud. "Why don't you just fill me in and I'll save myself the cost of a call." He looked at Tim.

"It is security matter, so I can't disclose details, but your help would be appreciated. Let's just say that I understand that, while you are a very successful businessman, you have political ambitions and will be running for office this time around?"

"That's correct."

"I do not wish to rake over the past, but perhaps you can recall a small indiscretion involving a hotel maid? The Deputy Director just wanted a brief word on the subject, to avoid any misunderstanding even though, it was a long time ago"

"I see. I would be only too happy to help out, a matter of National Security you say. I should consider it, not only an honour, but my duty. Get that estate agent in and we'll have the paper work sorted right now."

Tim was satisfied with the day's work, as he was driven back to Thames House. Three Russian scumbags housed, transport provided for them and they would not so much as be able to break wind without his knowing. He just needed the bastards to bite at the emails Harriet, Pelham and Levy were offering as bait.

Chapter 24

"There was no contact, that's why you have not spoken to Rafiq," said Denham. "Nothing since he dropped the girl at Calais. "

Tim was confused. He had expected to speak to Rafiq over two hours before and the call had not arrived. It was seven in the evening, the darkness outside his office turned the windows into mirrors. As he looked out, all he could see was the reflection of Denham, stood the other side of his desk and himself looking out. "He has made no contact?"

""None, I was against this from the start. Now we have no option, but to contact the French and tell them we have let a terrorist wander off in their Country. We had him Tim and you let the fucker slip through your fingers. Now the shit will hit the fan. We will look like total screw ups. I can't wait for the inquiry. There will be an inquiry, this Nizar was at the top and not just some deluded kid in his bedroom. He was a fully-fledged, fucking commander in Iraq."

Tim was trying to think. He had gambled on Nizar wanting to come in, then turn him and stop a major terror threat to the UK. It would have re-established their credibility. He had been certain. Had he blinded himself? He had been so sure. The Russians were personal, they had been responsible for the murder of his wife and he knew he was bending all the rules to get them to the UK where he could get to them. Nizar had been a judgment call and not a good one it appeared.

"He has not checked in? Is there anyway of contacting him?" said Tim.

"You know the protocol as well as I. Contacting an agent in the field is a basic no no. We have no way of knowing his situation, where he is or who he is with. What do we do, ring him? Picture the scene. He is surrounded by the opposition. The phone rings. "Hello this is MI5 here. How is it going?" Don't be so fucking stupid."

Tim knew Denham was right. Rafiq could have a thousand reasons for dropping off the grid. In any event, a phone call would probably not work. The phone Rafiq had used previously would have been disposed of after he had contacted MI5. He should have a new cell, so if he was taken, an inspection of his phone would reveal nothing.

Tim thought the logic through. He spoke his thoughts out loud. "Bear with me. After his conversation, in which we instructed him to put the girl on a coach to the UK, he was told to head south and he should have destroyed the phone used, correct?"

"So we have no way of contacting him or tracing him," said Denham.

Do we have his last cell number?"

"We can get it."

Here's my logic. We call him. If he no longer has the phone, we get no answer, obviously. If the phone is active, say for some reason and he still has it, as he did not have the opportunity to rid himself of it, then he may answer."

"There is the fucking obvious flaw. The only way he keeps the phone is that he did not have the chance to ditch it. You are looking at a single case scenario. He drops the girl off, drives away with Nizar and is taken as he heads from Calais."

"A possibility," said Tim.

"A more likely possibility is that his fucking passenger kills him and has it on his toes. You were wrong about this Nizar, just admit it and contact the French."

"We know that Rafiq saved Nizar and Aleena from a Jihadi hit man."

"Do we? What I actually know is that Rafiq catches up with the pair and stops Nizar from being topped. We only have Nizar's account. The other bloke is dead, shot by Rafiq. He could have told Rafiq a load of old toffee, His real intention may be to get to the UK to kill or bomb. You chose to believe his version. There are countless other possibilities."

"What about the girl? He seemed genuine in getting her back to her parents."

"How the fuck do I know? The point is that Rafiq called in for instructions, just to check, before calling in the French Security Service. You should have handed him in. We would not be in this bloody mess if you had listened in the first place."

"I know you don't think much of me," said Tim.

"No I don't, but that is not the issue. You shouldn't be in this job and my fears, that you would screw up and drag MI5 with you, seem to be confirmed. I care about what I do. I care about my Country and you are making the Service look incompetent. I am proud of what we do here keeping people safe. You, on the other hand seem to have no regard for anything, apart from your own agenda, whatever that is."

Tim knew Denham was right. He did have his own agenda. He was, however, doing his best to protect the UK, at the same time, he wanted the bastards that killed his wife brought to book. By serving himself, he was serving the Country by getting rid of them.

"If there is a major threat to the UK and all the evidence supports that, then taking a risk on Nizar was worth it. Countless lives could be saved," said Tim.

Denham took a deep breath and recovered his composure. "Well it hasn't worked out that way. We have lost an agent and an ISIS major league player is on the loose somewhere in Europe."

"Get me the number."

"Have you been listening to to what I have been saying?" said Denham.

"I heard you loud and clear. I remind you, I am still the boss here. Now get me the number, please."

Denham thought of saying something further, but knew disobeying a superior, would not be tolerated. Military Intelligence was what it said on the label. Its origins were firmly in the sphere of the army and one thing was self evident, disobeying a direct command only ended one way. That way would not be good for him. He gestured to the phone on Tim's desk. Tim waived his hand signalling for him to continue. He spoke and put the phone down.

****

Nizar had no idea what to do next. He had driven south and had turned off into a rest stop. The lay-by was surrounded by woodland and he had pulled off the road into an area where he would not be easily observed. He had spent the night sleeping in the car. It was only a matter of time before Rafiq and their two assailant's bodies were discovered. The Twingo would be traced to Rafiq and then the hunt would be on for him.

He had examined the phone he had retrieved from Rafiq's body. It was blank. Rafiq had deleted all the previous activity. He had been lucky so far. He had made it to France and Aleena was now, presumably, safely back in the UK with her parents. Now his luck had run out. He knew that Rafiq was to call and get instructions for their extraction and repatriation. He had no means of contact. He realised, that on the face of it, MI5 would be confronted with their agent's murder and his flight. Putting two and two together, it was obvious that he would be the prime suspect. Even if he could make contact with MI5, it was odds on that he was not going to be warmly welcomed.

He needed a piss. He opened the door of the BMW and wandered a few paces before opening his fly and beginning to urinate. The phone rang. It startled him and he pissed down his leg. "Fuck," he said, as he rushed back to the car to retrieve the phone.

"Hello," he said realizing it sounded pretty lame.

"Who's this?" said the voice on the other end.

Nizar was not sure how to respond. He finally said, "A friend of Rafiq's."

Tim looked at Denham, not sure what to say next.

Chapter 25

The Bombardier Learjet 85 taxied into the customs area at London City Airport. Vasiliev Nikhil, Sokolov Yerik and Volkov Lesta made their way to customs and immigration. Their journey from Moscow had been uneventful. They feared that, given their current relationship with the Russian establishment, there might have been some hindrance to their departure. They were both relieved and surprised when everything went smoothly.

They emerged from the airport to be met by AJ cars and joined the London traffic. The North Circular Road was slow moving, it took over two hours before they turned into the drive of their accommodation in Bishops Avenue.

The driver and the valet in residence moved their luggage from the car to their rooms. Having refreshed themselves, they met in the conservatory overlooking the garden and pool complex.

"What now?" said Nikhil?

"We wait. Graham and Mel said they would be right round. They are doing dinner here and we will discuss matters then," said Lesta.

"Do you think we could get some women to liven things up a bit?" suggested Nikhil.

"You are a dirty old fucker."

"Well, you need something to do to pass the time," said Nikhil.

"If you'd seen his wife you would want to make the most of being away from home," said Yerik.

"She's a lovely woman," replied Nikhil, "very clean."

"Clean!" said Lesta, "is that the best compliment you can pay her?"

"She likes cake," continued Nikhil.

"Well that's good then, clean and cake eating," said Yerik.

"Lots of cake "said Nikhil. "When I say cake, I mean she likes to eat. When I say, likes to eat, I mean she really likes to eat."

"She's fat is what you mean," laughed Yerik.

"It's her hobby. We all need a hobby. I screw prostitutes and she eats cake. What can I say," said Nikhil.

"I suppose it's better than fucking cake and eating prostitutes," said Lesta. They laughed.

"If she knew about them she might try eating them. I wouldn't put it past her. She'll put anything in her mouth she can get her hands on," said Nikhil.

"She puts everything in her mouth apart from your dick apparently, "said Yerik.

The translators listening to the conversation for MI5 laughed as well as they recorded and transcribed every word. Harriet, Pelham and Levy were gathered in Tim's office. The conversation was being relayed in real time to the screen on Tim's desk. Anything of significance would be flagged up and he would be alerted.

"So are you prepared?" asked Tim.

"We are meeting them around eight to lay the situation out," said Levy.

"We will present the Clinton emails as a money making opportunity on the currency markets. They are obviously interested in a Trump win, so they will make the running, with a bit of luck," said Pelham.

"Should be an easy sell"

"When do I come into play?" asked Harriet. She was clearly apprehensive at her role.

"We'll fix a meeting for tomorrow. You turn up with a sample or two of the emails from her aide and we negotiate a price. They just have to believe you are who you say you are and can deliver," said Levy.

"Stop worrying. Just be yourself," said Tim.

"We will do the talking," Pelham reassured her.

"Are you going to pick them up immediately?" said Harriet.

"No, I want more evidence before we move. I have their connection to money laundering documented, but what I really want is their complicity in trying to interfere in the US Presidential election and a link straight back to the Kremlin. I want to be able to arrest them, hold them and give the Americans enough to get an extradition warrant. I want them banged up for as long as possible and their assets seized globally, as the proceeds of their criminal activities. I want belt and braces on these bastards."

Pelham and Levy were taken aback by Tim's fervour. "That seems personal?" said Pelham.

It was very personal. These three men had caused the death of his wife and his best friend Harry Stiles. "Of course it was personal," he thought. He wanted these bastards burning in hell.

"Not personal," he lied. "They are indirectly funding terrorism.

They are laundering drug money. They are scum and I want them brought to book. That's all," said Tim.

The three people sat opposite him looked at each other. It was clear to them, despite Tim's statement, that he was heavily emotionally invested in bringing down the oligarchs. To them, it appeared that Tim exhibited the traits of a zealot. It worried them. If anything went wrong, they felt that things would not go well for them either.

Pelham and Levy needed immunity, without Tim they were both looking at financial ruin and major jail time. Harriet was concerned that Tim knew that she had co-operated with the former Boss of MI5 and spied on him. She did not need the head of the Service as her enemy.

"This is between us. You understand," Tim looked pointedly at Harriet. She knew at that point he knew and he was leaving her in no doubt. "I will bring in Denham, the FBI, the CIA, uncle Tom Cobbly and all when I have them by the short and curlies."

They all nodded and rose to leave.

"Get the bastards for me," was Tim's parting shot.

Chapter 26

The memories came flooding back as Tim drove into the car park at the Sovereign Harbour complex in Eastbourne. It was all so vivid in his mind. The marina surrounded by the blocks of flats, the small bridges connecting the walkways that circumnavigated the manmade harbour, the myriad of boats, small and large that bobbed gently in the breeze. All brought back the moment when he and Yosuf had first stepped ashore. It had only been a few months since he had arrived, on the run and hounded by ISIS.

In those months, so much had happened. Yosuf was dead. His wife was dead. Both the director and deputy director of MI5 were dead. He knew that there was more death to come. He was resigned to it. Death brought death. It was the way of things, not just in his life, but globally. Not a day passed it seemed without more deaths. The World was getting to be a far more dangerous place, terrorism and jingoism flourished. The conflicts in the Middle East were the catalyst that fuelled the instability.

He parked the car and made is way to the restaurant and retail area that bounded the North end of the harbour. It was cold and grey. It was two o'clock, but the light was already beginning to fade as a gentle mist rolled in from the sea and the drizzle began. He made his way past the various eateries to the Harvester Pub.

The pub was situated next to the small blue pedestrian bridge that had to be raised and lowered to allow the boats to pass through to the inner harbour. That part of the quay, to the left of the Harvester, was where the fishing boats moored. Tim walked past the pub entrance and looked to the spot where there were three or four boats that worked from the harbour, moored to unload their fish.

Two were still out. They would return soon. They did not fish in the dark. He retraced his steps and entered the pub. He ordered a coffee and sat at a table. After a few moments, the barmaid arrived with his espresso.

Getting here had been harder than he had thought it would be, not the drive, but ditching his ever-present bodyguards. Close personal protection had not been a feature of the job until he took the post as head of MI5. The Home Office felt that losing the Deputy Director was bad publicity, but having the Director turning up dead, was taking carelessness to a whole new level. When Tim took the post, he felt that he needed to a least stay alive for a bit, say at least until the next general Election, so he had accepted his shadows.

His bodyguards worked in shifts. There were supposed to be two bodyguards with him at all times. They were specially trained in personal protection by the police, a skill not present among MI5 operatives. Limited resources and the demands on the police had made the situation less and less viable as the weeks had progressed. There had to be compromises. Six officers could not been supplied all the time, so when the officers were needed elsewhere, MI5 agents were used.

Tim had been under MI5 protection today. He had engineered it that way. Now, having control over his protectors, he had told them to get on with something else useful, as he was going to be in the Office all day. He then just walked out of Thames house and taken the train to Gatwick, hired a car at the airport and driven to Eastbourne.

He sipped his coffee as he waited for the fishing boat to arrive. He didn't wait long. Twenty minutes later the pedestrian bridge was raised and the boat tied up. The fishermen began unloading their catch, which would be delivered to the wholesaler further along the coast towards Eastbourne Town Centre.

Tim sat watching the door to the Harvester. It opened and a rather tired man entered. He knew it was Nizar as soon as he stepped into the pub. The ethnicity of visitors and residents in Eastbourne was predominantly Caucasian, making him easy to spot. Nizar also had little difficulty in identifying Tim. He was the only person in the pub below retirement age.

"You made it," said Tim, as Nizar sat. Nazar nodded.

Tim knew the route Nizar had taken from France. He and Yosuf had arrived the same way. The Turks had their heroine importation supply line firmly established. A small boat would set off from the coast of France and meet with a fishing boat that operated out of a south coast port. They would transfer the heroine at sea. The boats would return to their respective ports in France and England having caught their fish. There was little chance of inspection. The length of the British and French coast meant there were nowhere near the resources available to realisticly man the whole of it.

Tim's visit to the Kebab shop in Wood Green, North London, had set up Nizar's extraction. The drug dealers had delivered his package to him. They had the same route that he and Yosuf had used to get out of France. He had given the instructions to Nizar on the phone to drive to Berk Plage, a small seaside resort on the coast in northern France, south of Calais. Tim's Turkish drug dealing friends were not stupid and had used the same route he had previously travelled. That way they, at least, limited the number of heroine supply routes, that were compromised, to one. Tim guessed that they would now close this route and move the importation of heroine to others.

"What happened to Rafiq?" asked Tim, having ordered some food from the counter and sat down again.

"He is dead. I am sorry. We were spotted, I think when we dropped the girl off at the bus departure point. They must have followed us out of Calais."

Tim took a deep breath. He knew that it would be down to him to explain the death of their son to Rafiq's parents, another pointless death. How he hated this man in front of him. So much pain and suffering in the name of religion. He betrayed none of his emotions. He needed Nizar for the moment if he was to prevent more deaths. Nizar needed to believe that he would be given a new life and a new identity if Tim was going to get his co-operation. First and foremost, he had to obtain the details of the imminent terrorist attack on the Capital and prevent it. Nizar was key to this, so Tim had no choice for the moment. Tim had no intention of letting Nizar escape justice. He would see him rot in hell, but not just yet. "Where are the bodies?" Tim asked.

"They are in a field in the hire car." Nizar went on to give Tim the full details and the location.

"I need to make a call," said Tim. Nizar looked panicked.

"You said that only you and I would be involved. I will tell you nothing until I have assurances that I shall be safe and immune from prosecution."

"It is not about you. It is about someone's son that is lying in a Field in France rotting." Tim walked outside and made his call. Within the hour, the French Police had located the bodies of Rafiq and the two Jihadis. At least Rafiq's parents would have their son's body to grieve over. Small consolation, as would be the medal and the letter that would accompany it. The son would be yet another unsung hero that had died for his Country.

"What now?"

"Now we go to my car and drive you to a hotel. Where you stay until I can organise things. No one but me will know your location.

You will go nowhere, nor contact anyone. Do you understand? " said Tim.

"I will do as you say."

"Understand me well. You will follow my instructions to the letter. I mean contact no one. Go nowhere or I will have you banged up until hell freezes over. Now how long do we have until the attack on London?"

"Two weeks"

Chapter 27

Tim looked at the news feed displayed on his laptop. It was the twenty seventh of October, just twelve days before the Americans were due to go to the ballot box to vote in a new President. The headlines showed the latest opinion polls and Hilary Clinton had a commanding lead over her rival Donald Trump. Tim took a deep breath before speaking to his secretary on the internal phone.

"Is my first conference call on schedule?"

His secretary's voice came through, "connecting now." The call was scrambled and secure.

"Hello Mr Director?" said Tim.

"Tim," said the Director of the CIA. "How are you?"

"I am good and you?"

"Good, good, what do have for me?"

"I have our Russian friends in a house in London."

"Excellent, I have the file and it gives us enough to go forward on the money laundering. Do you have more?"

"I will do in a few hours. Pelham, Levy and my agent will be meeting with them today and placing some documentation in their hands that will link them to a campaign to tamper with the US Presidential election."

"Hard evidence? We have lots of good intelligence to say that the Kremlin has been involved in all sorts of dirty tricks on the net, hacking into the Democrats campaign computers, bugging and checking emails. Physical proof would be the icing on the cake."

"I intend to give you Yerik, Lesta and Nikhil with their sticky fingers all over Hilary Clintons emails from her non sanctioned server."

"The FBI has already cleared her and they have been released on Wikileaks. That is not news my friend," said the Director.

"Not these emails, they are to her aide, Huma Abedin," said Tim.

"She was investigated and her tablet, mobile devices and computer were looked at by the FBI. They have already evaluated them, surely?"

"Not these, they were on Abedin's husband's computer, Anthony Weiner. They have come to light as part of the investigation into his so called sexting investigation."

"You are fucking kidding me. Are you sure?"

"I am very sure. I have copies of them all and our Russian friends will have them in a few hours. Is that enough for you to get your extradition warrant? Then you can bang the bastards up for a thousand years in the US?"

"Send me the evidence, with a link to the Russians and I'll get the warrant application process in motion," said The Director.

"How long?"

"It will take a couple of weeks."

"Fuck, they will be back in the bosom of mother Russia in a fortnight. Can't you expedite it?" said Tim.

"I will move as fast as I can. In the meantime you will have to keep them in the UK."

"I shall have to," Tim knew that he would do what was necessary to see them to justice. He would do what he had to do to stop the three men, responsible for Jackie's death, getting back to Russia.

"There is the matter of the emails?" said the Director.

"Leave it with me," said Tim.

"That, I can't do. It is a matter of US National Security. I am duty bound to act."

"I have a call booked with the FBI. As soon as you are off the air, I will convey the full facts to them. I will handle it. You have my words."

"Good enough, fuck I am glad I am not at the FBI. You are just about to ruin their day. They have already cleared Clinton in one investigation into her email activity. Now, you are about to dump a whole new pile of shit on them. The election is only just over a week away. The FBI is fucked whatever it does. Keep the new emails quiet and when she gets elected, what then? Start an investigation into the President Elect."

The alternative is just as bad. Reveal the new emails and the investigation now?" A week before the election. Whatever the outcome of the investigation, it would severely damage her chances of winning. What a fucking mess."

"I have to disclose what I have. There is no choice. I have to leave it to the FBI, otherwise MI5 would be in the shit, effectively, we would be interfering in the US democratic process if I withheld the information," said Tim.

"Good luck and good bye," said the Director.

Tim sat for a moment, following his conversation with the CIA. He was not bothered by the Americans problems. He was bothered by the Americans apparent tardiness in getting a warrant so he could drag the Russian bastards in. He made up his mind that whatever it took, they would not leave. They would get justice and he would get his revenge. They would not get back to the protection of their home Country. They would pay for Jackie's death. He would make sure of that, one way or another.

He sat quietly and calmed himself. He needed to focus and be dispassionate. He needed to be clear and calculating. He needed to ensure nothing was left to chance. He had his plan. He needed to stay with it, they would pay

Tim spoke to his secretary. Time to ruin someone's day, "Get me the FBI," he said.

Chapter 28

Denham and Tim sat in Tim's office. They were both concentrating on the audio playback. They were not only listening to the content of the conversation, but were trying to gauge the mood of the participants in the conversation.

Greetings were exchanged between Yerik, Nikhil, Lesta and their guest at the mansion in Bishops Avenue. Pelham and Levy could be heard enthusiastically reuniting with their clients. Then Harriet was introduced to the three Russians.

"This is Miss Shaw, the person we were telling about," said Pelham.

The Russians introduced themselves and Yerik took the lead in the conversation. Tim and Denham had heard enough surveillance tapes to be able to recognise the individual voices of the participants now. In any event, each had the typed transcript of the full conversation in front of them, with a translation of any parts spoken in Russian. "Welcome Miss Shaw, tell me a little about yourself."

There was a pause and finally Harriet spoke. "There's nothing to tell. I have something that you want and Mr Pelham tells me that you will pay for it."

"Yes we shall, but first I should like you to clarify a few matters for us. While we trust Mr Pelham and of course Mr Levy, having done business with them on numerous occasions, we know nothing about you. That being the case, would you tell me how you and Mr Pelham know each other?"

"It is a long story," began Harriet.

"We have time."

"Ok, he is my Godfather and he used to work with my father who was an accountant."

Pelham interrupted, "Richard, Harriet's dad and I worked together over a number of years. We concentrated on selling tax planning. He worked in the city of London and I handled some of the off shore work."

"Anyway he worked with my Dad," continued Harriet. "When my dad died he helped my mum out."

"How did your father die?" said Lesta.

"Cancer, nothing dramatic," said Harriet

"Continue," said Yerik.

"I graduated and was eventually recruited by MI5. We kept in touch and I just happened to mention the tapes."

"Why would you do that?" Surely they are a secret," said Nikhil.

"I accept that it was not very discreet of me. However I do not see many honest men in this room who should be passing judgement on me," said Harriet.

Listening to the tape, Denham let out a grunt. "Good attack is always a sound tactic."

"The cover story seems to be holding as well," said Tim.

They continued to listen to the exchange as Harriet continued.

"The emails are in the possession of the American court system, they are not just yet public knowledge. I am not giving up secrets. From what I understand from Mr Pelham and Mr Levy, the key factor is, when the emails are made public. If you gentleman have them, you will have that control."

"Release them now and they would severely damage Hilary Clinton's chance of winning. She is odds on to win. That would change in an instant with these further revelations. There is a lot of money to be made in the markets. Timing is always key. Anyone can predict a rise or a fall, but the when is the hard part. These emails give you the when," said Levy.

"Do you have them?"

"Here is a sample," said Harriet

There was silence on the tape and a discussion in Russian. Tim and Denham looked down at their written transcripts. "They look genuine," said voice one.

"There are undoubtedly genuine," said voice two.

"We can make some money and get ourselves out the shit with the Kremlin," said voice one.

"It will cost. Levy and Pelham will want theirs on top of what the girl wants." Said voice three.

"We need it and we could make some money on the markets. Stop fucking about. Get the rest of them and get them to the Kremlin. We will be off the hook and life goes on. Otherwise it is only a matter of time until we end up in prison for some trumped up charge." Said voice two.

"We would like the emails, how much?" said Yerik.

"Ten million dollars," said Levy.

"Too much," said Nikhil.

"Take it or leave it." They heard Harriet's voice on the audio.

"Jesus," said Denham "she's getting carried away with the role."

"She's good, bloody good," said Tim.

"OK, when and how?" said Yerik.

There was an audible collective sigh of relief from Tim and Denham.

"Now, and you transfer the money to a designated account electronically and the emails will be sent electronically to you. I should warn you, there are thousands of them." Said Levy.

"Fuck, she's done it," said Denham, as they listened to the transaction being completed.

"Get the audio to the CIA and the let's hope they now have enough to get those Russian bastards extradited to the States. Tell them to get a move on before they jump on the private Jet back to Moscow," said Tim.

Chapter 29

Aleena's operation went well and she was now ready to travel back to her home in Walsall. Tim had arranged that no charges were brought against her and her passport was returned. The press had been leaked her story. The Government had seen it as an ideal opportunity to dissuade other would be radicals following in her shoes. It was also good anti ISIS propaganda. The opportunity had been too good to pass up. Aleena was now notorious, with millions having read her story.

Tim had made a final gesture and organised a private ambulance for her, paid for by MI5, to transport her home. She felt depressed as she got herself dressed and was wheeled down to the waiting ambulance. She had not been visited by her Mother, Father or brother during her stay in hospital. The clothes she wore were not her own and had been cobbled together by the hospital.

The journey back home gave her ample time to reflect. The cold damp streets and the autumn green of the trees were in stark contrast to the arid browns of her previous environs. They were different worlds, neither perfect, but both capable of innate beauty and both subject to human corruption. She saw that, irrespective of faith, all people were capable of selfless acts of good and callous acts of evil.

As she watched the motorway junction markers roll by from the window and her destination coming ever closer, she began to worry. She worried that none of her family had visited her in hospital. It was a bit of a journey, but they had a car and there were trains. She worried about the press coverage and how she would resume her life. She worried about the death of her sister and her friend. She worried that maybe ISIS would seek some sort of retribution on her for fleeing their cause.

Her trepidation grew stronger as the ambulance turned into the Victorian terrace where her family home was situated. The ambulance stopped in front of the house and the driver exited and rang the front door bell. Aleena watched anxiously as the driver waited for a response. Finally, her Mother opened the door.

Her Mother stepped into the street and looked up and down the road in both directions. Aleena for the first time became aware of the eyes looking from doors and windows. Curtains were being lifted and it was clear that the appearance of the ambulance had triggered a flurry of neighbourly activity, centred on her family home.

Her Mother retreated back into the house, while the driver opened the rear doors to the van. The nurse, that had travelled with her, pushed her wheel chair onto the ramp at the rear and the driver operated the mechanism that lowered her to ground level. She could walk, but until she had time to heal further, the hospital recommended she did not over exert. Ideally, they had wanted her to stay a few more days, but she had been eager to return home. Now, she was feeling less sure about her decision.

The door to the house closed behind her and the nurse and driver departed. Her Mother stood before her.

"Mother" said Aleena tearfully.

Her Mother seemed unsure what to do or say. Finally, she stirred. "Are you hungry?"

Aleena was confused. No kiss, no hug, and no warmth, it was strangely formal. "Mother," She repeated.

131

Her Mother said nothing and pushed the wheelchair into the lounge. There was some comfort in the familiar surroundings, the wall covering, the black and white photos of her Father and his family in the village in Pakistan, the cushions on the floor and the smell of her Mother's cooking. It was home. Why did she not feel the warmth of home?

"Talk to me Mummy," said Aleena.

"Are you ok?"

"I will recover," it was so distant, Aleena struggled with her Mother's formality. She tried again. "Where are Papi and Imran?" Imran was her elder brother.

"At the Mosque."

"Prayers are not today. Why have they gone to the Mosque? Did they not know I was coming home?"

"It is difficult. They are seeking guidance. They will be back soon." Her Mother seemed embarrassed and left the room and busied herself in the kitchen preparing lunch.

Aleena sat and waited. Time seemed to stand still. She had not thought of such a moment as this, when she, her sister and friend left to go to Turkey and there to join the glorious soldiers of the caliphate. She had seen herself as a heroine. She would be the bride of a brave soldier in the army of Islam. They had not been taken as noble daughters of the revolution and brides of the brave. They had been used as the camp whores.

Now, sitting broken, mentally and physically, the truth dawned. She was an embarrassment to her family. No longer a virgin, no longer capable of bearing children and diseased, she was a source of shame and dishonour. She no longer belonged.

She heard the front door opening and her Father and brother

132

enter the house. They stopped talking and entered the room, where she waited. Her Father stood before her, just looking. Her brother joined him and stood.

"Papi," she said, looking for love, a sign of affection.

He just turned, left the room and joined her Mother in the kitchen. She heard him say." I cannot bring myself to even look upon her, the shame and the dishonour. I never thought there would be a day like this in my family."

Aleena felt the tears run down her cheeks. She looked pleadingly at her brother for solace. He stared back with only a look of disgust and disdain, wrritten large across his face. There was silence, a thick dark intimidating silence, the sort of silence that follows the flash of lightening before the sudden clap of the thunder that follows and shakes the air itself.

"Better you were dead," he said, turned his back and left the room.

Chapter 30

Tim's call to the Director of the FBI certainly put the cat among the pigeons. The full text of his letter to Congress was all across the media. Tim was displaying it on his screen. It read:

"In previous congressional testimony, I referred to the fact that the Federal Bureau of Investigation (FBI) had completed its investigation of former Secretary Clinton's personal email server. Due to recent developments, I am writing to supplement my previous testimony.

In connection with an unrelated case, the FBI has learned of the existence of emails that appear pertinent to the investigation. I am writing to inform you that the investigative team briefed me yesterday, and that the FBI would take appropriate investigative steps designed to allow investigators to review the emails to determine whether they contain classified information, as well as to asses their importance to our investigation.

Although the FBI cannot assess whether or not this material may be significant and I cannot predict how long it will take us to complete this additional work, I believe it is important to update your Committee about our efforts, in light of my previous testimony."

It was signed by the Director of the FBI.

Denham finished reading and turned the screen on Tim's desk so it now faced him. "Bugger me. Do you think you prompted this?"

"I doubt it. The FBI is not stupid, they were probably aware of the emails but undecided what to do. They are between a rock and a hard place. If they did nothing and Clinton was elected, they would be investigating the new President and if there was any wrongdoing, they would be accused of withholding information and so aiding her election. If they, as they have done, reopen the investigation, they stand accused of damaging Clinton if nothing comes from it. Either way they were fucked."

"What are our Russian friends doing?"

"Two guesses," said Tim.

"Getting pissed and celebrating?"

"You got it in one. Now our problem is that the bastards will fly off back to Mother Russia and out of our jurisdiction."

"Do we know from the bugs in the house if they have made plans/"

Tim pressed a few keys on his computer and the latest transcripts of the conversations in the house, where the three were staying, came up. The translators were only sending, via the feed, edited highlights. "They are planning to return on Friday week in their private Jet," said Tim.

"Waiting for the US presidential results, makes sense. If Trump gets elected, there will be rejoicing in the Kremlin and our three will be top flavour of the month and in everyone's good books. It will be back to business as usual for them."

Without an extradition request from the US, we cannot do anything and they walk free."

"It is progressing, but at its own pace. They think they will be in a position to apply in about eight days."

"That's no fucking good. That will be the Friday they will fly out and it will be too late," said Tim.

"Can't we arrest them on some pretence?" said Denham.

"That would tip our hand. At the end of the day, they are supposedly legitimate bankers. A trumped up charge and a false arrest would hardly fair well at an extradition hearing and they would get off with a smart lawyer. I have checked with legal and they don't recommend it."

"What do we do then? Just watch them fly off into the sunset."

"You do nothing. I will fuck up their travel plans," said Tim.

"You don't want to know, but I am not letting these wankers out of my grasp. Trust me I shall do whatever it takes to get them."

Denham frowned and considered the matter. He had no love for Tim and wanted nothing more than to see him fall flat on his face. On the other hand, MI5 had been under the cosh so much recently that he did not want any further scandals heaped on it. A rogue head of the service breaking the law would not serve his purpose. He wanted Tim gone. He wanted his job. He did not want MI5 reduced to a basket case.

"Don't do anything rash," he cautioned.

"It won't be rash. It will be considered and then I'll blow their brains out with my own hands if I have to," said Tim.

Denham now realised that Tim was serious. He needed to think his response. Should he go over Tim's head to the Home Secretary? It was difficult. It would not improve his standing one jot if he was seen to be disloyal to his boss. There was one thing you never did in the Civil Service and that was to undermine those above you. The mandarins were a tight knit group and backed each other. They controlled the Knighthoods and the promotions. Break rank and

136

there were so many ways that you could falter. You were one of them or you were on the outside. You were the "right sort" or you were not part of their club. For the moment, Denham would wait and hope that Tim took enough rope to hang himself.

Tim knew full well that Denham itched to replace him. He also knew he did not give a flying fuck. Those Russians had killed his wife, his best friend and led to the suicide of his former boss. They dripped blood from their avaricious hands. He would have no hesitation, given the chance, of making them pay for their greed.

In the meantime, we wait and see how the extradition proceedings progress," said Tim.

That was a further point of unrest between Tim and Denham. "Where is Nizar? I know that you disappeared and no one knows where you went. Have you got him back in the UK? "

"I have employed him as an informant effectively and so, he will be immune from prosecution because he was working for us in Iraq and Syria as an agent."

"You and I know that is just not true," said Denham.

"I will give him a letter to that effect."

"You are helping a high tanking ISIS member to evade justice."

"I can't put right what has been done, but I can save countless lives in the future. What other way would he be willing to give up the details of the latest attack planned in London. What incentive does he have if he is facing life in prison?"

"That is not the point."

"What other point is there? I can't stop the killing in the Middle East, but I can prevent it on the streets of the UK. One terrorist getting off for acts, not even committed in this Country against the lives of everyday people going about their business, is not hard to justify, is it?"

"I see the logic and I understand, but it is our role to uphold the law, not aide in its breaking," said Denham.

"Tell that to the relatives of the dead and maimed by yet another bomb going off. I am not asking you to go along with it. I am asking you to do nothing. It is all on my back and you need know nothing unless you choose. You have no idea where this Nizar is. All you know is that he is helping us to stop a terrorist attack. Leave it at that and leave the moral dilemma to me."

Denham rose from his seat and shaking his head, left the room. "Enough rope," he thought as he closed the door," just enough rope."

Chapter 31

Nizar was getting jumpy, alone in the safe house. He had heard nothing from Tim over the last week and had not left the house. Food appeared by supermarket home delivery and was suited to his religious affiliation being Halal. He had the television, but no phone or internet. Tim had taken his mobile phone. He had considered purchasing another, but he also knew that making phone calls could, potentially, lead to him being traced by ISIS. In any event, he had no one he wanted to phone other than his mother and he felt certain that her phone had been monitored since the day he and his brother travelled to Syria for training. He would have just to wait it out and rely on Tim.

The doorbell rang and then the door began to open. For a brief moment, he felt panic. Then his brain engaged and realised that only MI5 had keys. Tim stepped through the door. "How are you?" was Tim's first question.

Nizar did not need to answer. Tim could see a man that was stressed and agitated. He was pleased to see that the once tough Jihadi was buckling under the simple strategy of just leaving him on his own with his thoughts. Uncertainty and isolation is a powerful force on the mind, of even the strongest individual. Tim needed Nizar to be dependent on him for everything. He wanted him to take instruction and comply without questioning.

Tim needed Nizar to work with him of his own accord and not just be co-erced or bribed with a promise of immunity from prosecution. He wanted Nizar to be what he was on paper, a MI5 informant. MI5 had turned many spies in the cold war. The only difference was that Nizar had been turned from ISIS and not the Russians.

"I'm ok, but I was concerned at not being contacted for so long."

"There are more things in the World than you. I am a busy man and my colleagues are not as keen on saving you from prison as I seem to be. The more moderate of them would offer charges that carry a ten year tariff in return for you cooperation rather than life."

"And the less moderate?"

"Rendition, a quite trip abroad, so to speak and a bit of water boarding."

Tim watched as Nizar adjusted to the threat element in their relationship. Nizar was battle hardened and had seen it all, but Tim could see the cracks appearing in him. The isolation had exposed the effects of prolonged combat on the man. In the past it had been called shellshock, now post traumatic stress.

"Don't worry. I am a man of my word. You just need to demonstrate to me that you are fully cooperating. You understand?"

Nizar nodded his head in compliance. "Would you like tea or coffee?" He returned having made them both coffee and sat on the sofa facing Tim, who had taken up the armchair opposite.

"Let's start with everything you know about Iraq and Syria. I want as much detail as you can give me on ISIS, personnel, chain of command, supply routes, intelligence. Give me as much detail as you can recall." Tim switched on the recorder he had placed on the coffee table that was situated between them.

Over the lunch break, Tim judged that Nizar was being truthful and compliant. Satisfied that he was imparting valuable intelligence and more to the point, reliable intelligence, he knew that it was safe to hand the debriefing over. In any event, Tim needed to return to Thames House.

The doorbell rang. Nizar started. "It is a colleague who will continue the debriefing over the next few days," said Tim, as he got up to answer the door.

"This is Harriet Shaw. She will continue with you."

Tim had selected Harriet to keep it low key and from Denham's scrutiny. As far as Denham was concerned, she was still liaising with Pelham, Levy and the three Russians. In fact, Tim had let Levy go back to the USA, with his immunity from prosecution, to help the lawyers build their case for extradition against the Russians. Pelham had also gone to the states to aid the cause.

Time was running out. It was Tuesday and the election was on Thursday. The Russians were staying until Friday. Their private jet was at London City airport, waiting to take them back. If Trump won the US Presidency, they planned to return to Moscow, fully reinstated as the Kremlin's favourite oligarchs. Tim needed the Americans to get the request for extradition to the UK by the weekend, or the Russians would be out of reach.

Tim put that to the back of his mind and turned his attention back to Nizar. Harriet had taken control of the recorder and would have the conversations transcribed later.

"Tell me about the planned attack in London before I go," he said.

Nizar knew that this was his Ace in the hole, his guarantee of safety. "You promised me a letter," he said.

Tim allowed the tension to build briefly, sitting silently, scrutinising Nizar. It was merely theatre on his part. Nizar was fully cooperating and had already given Tim a vast amount of invaluable intelligence in the one short debriefing session they had had that morning.

Tim made great play of opening his jacket pocket and removing the envelope. He placed it on the table between them, "your get out of jail free card."

Nizar looked at the envelope. He could not resist. Like a greedy child who just had the sweet jar put before him, he instantly picked it up. He opened it and read. He was satisfied and looked up at Tim and Harriet.

"It is planned for this Sunday, Remembrance Sunday. They are going to blow up the Cenotaph in Whitehall."

Every year a remembrance service is held at the Cenotaph in London. The Royal Family attends, along with current and past Prime Ministers, leading politicians, the heads of the armed services, the police chief along with veterans of the various conflicts in which they fought for their Country. It is celebrated on the nearest Sunday after the eleventh day, of the eleventh month, at eleven o'clock. The day the hostilities ceased in the Great War. Two minutes silence is observed throughout the United Kingdom to remember the fallen.

Tim knew that such an attack had always been on the agenda for the terrorists. The security was, however, daunting and a great hindrance to the execution of any would be bomber.

Nizar continued, "It has been months in the planning." He went on to reveal how Jimmy Buari and Sinita had befriended Charlie Wicks, a wheelchair bound war veteran who was due to be on parade. How he was to be the unwitting bomber with his new wheel chair, supplied by Buari, containing the bomb.

"How do you contact Buari?" asked Tim.

"I have a phone number. He is waiting on me for the go ahead."

"What happens if he doesn't hear from you?"

"He will either go ahead, attack the Cenotaph, or he may just select a softer target."

Tim left knowing that time was running out. Two days until the US elections, three until the Russians were out of his reach and five days until the worst terrorist attack in UK history.

Chapter 32

"You represent the best of America and being your candidate has been one of the greatest honours of my life," Clinton said. "I know how disappointed you feel, because I feel it too and so do tens of millions of Americans who invested their hopes," It was Wednesday morning in New York and it was with these words that she conceded defeat in the race to the White House.

Tim listened to the audio of the three Russians celebrating in the house in North London. There was little need for the translation transcripts, their jubilation was self-evident.

There were phone calls to Moscow. The Russians were overjoyed that Trump was the New President elect. They saw him as their man. He had, after all, already signalled his admiration for Vladimir Putin. Now he was the President of the US and the leader of the Free World. It was clear from the phone calls that, not only had Yerik, Nikhil and Lesta been doing their utmost to help Trump's cause, but the Russian Secret service had been on the job as well, hacking computers and throwing dirt at Clinton.

Tim picked up the phone and called for his Deputy to come up. As he waited for Denham to arrive, he realised that the three Oligarchs would depart in a couple of days and return home with their power and influence increased. He could see his chances of avenging his wife, Jackie's, death rapidly fading.

There was a knock and Denham walked in. He looked tired and Tim assumed that like him, he had stayed up most of the night watching the election. It was now afternoon in the UK and the morning after in the US.

"The Russians are they still celebrating?" he asked, as he made himself comfortable in the chair by Tim's coffee table, opposite Tim. He reached forward and poured himself a cup of coffee from the pot sitting on the table.

"Drunk as skunks and happy as pigs in shit," said Tim.

"Send the tapes of their conversations and their celebrations to the CIA. At least they will have proof of the extent the Russians were involved in attempts to influence the outcome, if they don't have it already."

Denham nodded. The tapes, along with other evidence, were, unknown at the time to Tim and Denham, to become part of a major row between President Elect Trump and his own security services. It would, by January the following year, lead to Trump, in effect, disbelieving his own Countries Intelligence Services and questioning their motives.

"What now?" said Denham?

"Have the Americans prepared their paper work for the arrest of the Russian bustards?"

"No chance."

"So, they will finish the partying, sober up, get on their plane and be on their way back to Russia and we can do sod all about it?"

"There will be another chance. I am sure," said Denham.

"I am not," Tim was agonising at the thought of his wife's killers merrily carrying on with their lives.

"Well, what can we do?"

"One thing I do know, is that I am not going to let them just fly off into the sunset, Scott free."

"Don't do anything rash. We have no reason to hold them under English law. You don't want to spark an International incident. I don't understand why you are taking it all so personally? After all, the World is full of dodgy bankers, financiers and gun runners. Why are you fixated with this particular group of tossers?"

Tim could not answer that question. "It pisses me off, that's all," he said.

"Fair enough, so what about this Nizar chap, who you are keeping so close to your chest?" Where are we at with that?"

"Tim stood up and walked up to his desk. He picked up the file marked "Top Secret" and returning to his seat handed it to Denham.

He opened the file and started to read. Tim sat watching in silence as Denham's eyebrows went up and down, interrupted by some brow furrowing. The information was of the first order, giving insight and details of ISIS activities, command and control and operational strength and targets.

"This is good stuff. It looks like your unorthodox method in getting hold of him has paid dividends."

The file that Tim had presented was incomplete. He had removed all and every detail of the plot to bomb the Cenotaph that Sunday. "I need you to share this with the CIA and our NATO allies. This should help in Iraq and Syria, save a few lives at least."

"I'll get it into the right hands. Leave it to me. It should get us some well-earned brownie points with the Americans, at least. Now, have you found out about the planned target in the UK?"

"He's withholding that for the present," Tim lied.

"Are you going to give him the letter you promised?"

"It is difficult."

"It is more than difficult. You are effectively letting a known ISIS leader and international terrorist walk free. More to the point, you are aiding him by giving him the cover story of being an MI5 undercover operative."

"Leave it with me."

"I am not sure I can. I will be no part of breaking the law. You can't ask me to do that."

"I won't. Just do nothing, that is all I ask at this juncture. I shall bear the sole responsibility and make it clear that you had no knowledge of what I was up to."

Denham sat quietly, having made a decision he spoke. "I think I will have to consult with the Home Secretary."

"You'll go ever my head?"

"I have my duty. You leave me no choice."

"If you say so, when."

"Monday," he got up and left.

Time was running out for Tim.

Chapter 33

The security at City Airport in London's Docklands was always tight. The Avolux engineers however, were waved through. Although it was three in the morning, Friday, there was nothing suspicious in engineers arriving to repair an aircraft. Parts were flown to the UK from all over the World and when they arrived, they were usually fitted quickly. Aircraft on the ground did not make money for the operators, so getting them air worthy and flying was always a priority, working overnight was common.

The three workmen soon located the Bombardier Learjet. Seventy million dollars or more, with extras, of aircraft belonging to the Baltic Bank and used by the three Russians to take them on their little jaunts around the Globe. They soon located the head of maintenance for the hanger who was on duty that night.

"I have nothing scheduled, "said the supervisor looking in his log.

One of the three stepped forward. "I need you to cooperate fully."

The supervisor, who had up to this point been doing nothing more than playing on his game consul, suddenly began to pay attention." I don't understand."

"I am a member of Her Majesty's Security Service," he produced his warrant card and showed it to the supervisor. The two Avolux engineers stood silently behind them.

"You are a spy, like James Bond?"

The MI5 officer repressed a smile. He wished, fast cars and even faster women. He spent most of his time in an office looking at people's life histories and doing background checks. This was the closest he had got to actual physical counter espionage in all that time. "MI6," he said.

"I don't understand," said the supervisor.

"James Bond is with MI6. I am with MI5."

"Right," replied the supervisor, now looking more confused than before.

"My colleagues and I need access to an aircraft."

"That's no problem. I just need to see the authorisation, the details of the certificate qualifying you to work on the type of aircraft and a maintenance order signed by the owner. I'll log it and you are free to start work."

"I can see that you are highly trained and dedicated and appreciate your devotion to duty. There is however one small problem. We don't have any of the bits of paper that would authorise us to work on the Learjet in question."

"What do you want me to do? I can't let people just wander in and play with the planes, can I?"

"Of course not, but you can comply with a request from MI5."

Confusion spread rapidly across the supervisors face. "I think I need to phone my boss." He started to walk back into his office in the corner of the hanger. The office was built in to one corner and consisted of two half-glazed wall panels and a door. Inside was the computer, phone, shelves with aircraft manuals, a couple of worn chairs and a desk stacked high with paper.

"I rather you didn't do that." The Agent stepped in front of the man and blocked his path. "I want you to take a moment and think about this. MI5 is asking you for your cooperation and you are turning us down. I want you to ask yourself one question."

"What's that?"

"How would you like for me to arrest you on suspicion of terrorism and keep you somewhere nice and quiet for the next few days?"

"You can't do that. I have rights."

"Of course you do. We all have rights. The difference is that I have the power to enforce them and you will have seventy-two hours locked up to think about yours. All I am asking is that you help your Country fight the bad guys. The alternative is that you will be obstructing us and we will do what we have to anyway and keep you out of the way for a bit."

"How can I help?"

"First forget we were ever here. Don't log it. Don't tell anyone. Do not speak to the pilots when they turn up. Is that clear? "

"Alright, I can do that. Follow me."

"Just one more thing, I am handing you this notification."

"What is it?"

"Just so you know you are bound by the Official Secrets Act. If you ever speak of this, it just lets you know you have committed an offence and go to prison, just a formality of course."

He took the notice and showed them to the oligarchs plane. He then disappeared into his office and resumed his game on the X-Box.

The engineers set to work. It took less time than the MI5 agent thought." Done, this plane is going nowhere until Sunday, at least," said one of them.

"What did you do?"

"I fucked up the altimeter. I checked the availability and it will take until Saturday night, at the earliest, to get a replacement."

"And I shoved a screwdriver into the starter circuit so it won't fire up. Not subtle, but effective. It is not going anywhere for a bit."

"Did you really shove a screwdriver in it?" asked the agent in disbelief.

"Metaphorically, it will light up like a Christmas tree with warning lights when the pre-flight checks are run, but there is no real damage. It will take ages to trace it all though and declare it safe to fly."

Chapter 34

Uncle Mas was driving the four by four. Aleena was still not completely recovered from her operation, her parents had felt it best that she completed her recuperation in Pakistan with her father's family. Aleena had never met "Uncle Mas" before. He was definitely some sort of relative, perhaps her father's cousin or second or third cousin. Leaving Heathrow on her own had been upsetting. Neither her Mother nor Father had seen her off. Her brother had left her in the check in queue with out waiting to see her go through to departures.

She had feared that she would be detained, but it was clear that Nizar's deal with MI5 had held good and she was allowed through without incident. The flight had seemed endless and she arrived exhausted and disorientated. The airport was overcrowded and chaotic. She was almost in a state of collapse as she walked from the arrivals area and saw her name on a piece of cardboard being held aloft by a middle-aged man, dressed in traditional tribal garb.

This was Uncle Mas. He was a complete stranger to Aleena, but she had no choice but to follow him to the beaten up old truck. She joined him in the cab, while her luggage, a single case was thrown in the rear. The truck stank. She recognised the smell. She had smelt it before in the trucks ISIS had used to move her around, a mixture of human sweat and goat or sheep excrement.

It was crowded and disorganised, people and vehicles were going in all directions. She felt sick. The truck seemed to have no suspension and the roads got worse the further they went and the closer they travelled into Kohistan. She had googled Kohistan and found that it was in the northwest of the Country. It was poor, rugged and tribal.

The progress was slow and she was in pain. The healing process, following her operation, was not complete and the dehydration from the long flight, coupled with the poor suspension of the vehicle, made her fell worse and worse as the journey progressed. It seemed endless. Her companion, barely spoke. There was no warmth or friendship. He hadn't even asked about Aleena's father, to whom he was supposed to be related. He had not asked about England or her journey. She tried to engage him in conversation, but his replies were curt and unhelpful.

"How far is the village?" she asked.

"A while yet," was the reply.

"How long since you have seen my Father?"

"Before you were born."

He said no more and they travelled in silence. The terrain became hasher and more mountainous. The villages they passed through were drab and the inhabitants poorly dressed. The region was one of the poorest areas of Pakistan. The people survived on subsistence agriculture and keeping animals. It had the lowest literacy rate in the country, with less tan ten percent of its population able to read. The rate amongst the women and girls was nearer one hundred percent.

The province was, more or less, beyond the reach of the law and the police. The area was controlled by the religious leaders and the tribal elders. The tribal councils, known as "Jirgas", held sway over the poverty struck and uneducated Muslim villagers. The Jirga leaders would go to any lengths to keep control and resist any attempts by the authorities to impose the rule of law. They defied any attempt to give women any rights, virtually considering them

153

worthless.

After hours of driving, the truck stopped in the village. Aleena stepped from the truck and found herself surrounded by what seemed the entire village. About thirty or forty people had gathered. No one greeted her. She seemed to be an object on display. There was hushed conversations and comments that were directed at her. She had trouble understanding the local dialect, but it was clear, they were not warm words of welcome.

Aleena had stayed in some dumps during her time with ISIS fighters. The hovel she was pushed through the door to, ranked right up there with the best of them. She found herself in the semi darkness, sat on a compacted mud floor, with a straw mattress in one corner and nothing else. The woman had, more or less, just pushed her into the cell before giving her a glowering look and retreating into an another room.

This village, unbeknown to Aleena had been investigated several times over the last seven years by the authorities. Three girls had gone missing. They were known as Bazeegha Sareen Jan, Begum Jan Amina and Shaheen. They had last been seen alive here. Their fate was still a mystery.

The investigation of their disappearance was hampered by cultural taboos, a lack of official will, local leaders putting up a wall of silence and a total lack of co-operation by the villagers. The religious leaders were suspected of ordering their deaths and the families had carried out their instructions.

Their fates have been shrouded by cultural taboos, official inertia, implacable resistance from local elders and religious leaders suspected of ordering their deaths, and elaborate subterfuges by the families, who reportedly carried out those orders.

Hundreds of so-called "honour killings" take place every year. The disgraced girls were imprisoned by their family members for weeks.

They had boiling water thrown on them and hot coals. The family then killed them and buried them in the hills.

They had brought dishonour to there families, Aleena had brought dishonour to her family.

Chapter 35

Tim, Denham and Harriet were gathered in Tim's office in Thames House. It was late and the winter nights were beginning to draw in. The chill was not, however. just outside on the streets of London, there was an icy atmosphere in the room as well. Denham had an expression that was reminiscent of someone who had just bitten into a lemon. Harriet was looking confused and unhappy. Tim, in contrast, was displaying an air of total indifference.

"Their plane just conveniently broke?" said Denham.

"It would appear so. That was a bit of luck for us wasn't it?" said Tim.

"You are fucking unbelievable. Words fail me. You are supposed to be enforcing law and order, not breaking every one you can think of. You had their plane sabotaged, didn't you?"

"It is good news though. The Russians are stuck her until Sunday at least," said Harriet.

"Please shut up," Denham said to Harriet. Turning his attention back to Tim, he said, "I asked you a question."

"You seem a little confused here. If I remember rightly, I am the head of MI5 and I think you'll find I ask the questions and you answer them, not the other way round," said Tim.

Denham was seething, but realised he could do very little at present. He would investigate and make sure he put together the who and the when of what happened to the Russian's Learjet and ensure he tied it back to Tim. He would have to wait his time beyond that.

"The request for extradition?" Tim asked Harriet.

"Stalled, ground to a halt, they just don't seem to have the will. They will all be replaced in a few months when Trump picks his new team. So there is no incentive to dig into a pile of crap. In any event, Trump seems far more favourabley disposed to Russia and there is even talk of the removal of sanctions."

"If the sanctions are lifted, then half the case against the Russians becomes academic," said Denham.

Despite Tim's best efforts, it looked like the bastards that killed his wife were just going to get on a plane on Sunday afternoon, fly off into the sunset and live happily every after. He could not let that happen.

"Fuck it," said Tim in frustration. "Get out both of you."

Tim sat in silence for a long while and thought. He wanted them dead. He had never killed anybody in his life. He had been close on two occasions. On both occasions, fate had intervened. He could not rely on fate on this occasion. He opened his desk. He removed an old book in Arabic, a gift from a friend. He turned to the page, well thumbed, showing the Gods judging the souls of the dead. They weighed them against a feather. Those without sin weighed less and passed into the after life. Those failing were eaten by the Crocodile God, Sobek.

He pulled the second item from his draw. It was the Makarov pistol, the untraceable gun given to him by Yosuf. He stared at both for a long time. He thought. He knew this was a turning point. He hesitated. Then he resolved his conflicts. He turned to the last page of the book and there were several small feathers. He removed three, before putting the book back into the draw. They were the

157

weights against which Nikhil, Lesta and Yerik's souls had been weighed.

Tim checked the Makarov and made sure it was loaded. He did not return it to the draw, but put it in his jacket pocket. He left his office, putting the lights out and locked the door. He felt finality as the key turned in the lock. His anger and hatred for the three oligarchs had transformed within to a cold inevitability. Time had run out and death was written large in the pages of the book and in his heart. He would ensure that Sobek had his last meal and that Annubis would live one more time.

Chapter 36

Sunday November thirteenth, Charlie Wicks woke early and excited. It was a crisp cold morning and rain was not forecast for Central London. It was a struggle to get up, wash and shave without the aid of his career, but he persevered. By seven o'clock, he had eaten and was dressed in his black trousers, blue blazer and his black shoes were so brightly polished, he could literally see his face in them.

The finishing touch was pinning on his medals. He took great care to ensure they were perfectly in a line, at just the correct height on the left breast of his jacket. He managed to manoeuvre himself to the hallway where he could view himself in the full-length mirror, that was attached to the wall. He was really pleased with his new wheelchair. It had been delivered yesterday. It was the top of the range and compared to the wobbly, squeaky and heavy previous version, it was a marvel of modern engineering. He was amazed at the kindness of total strangers. The generosity of the gift of this wheelchair meant so much to him. Without it, he would have been unable to take part in the ex-servicemen's Remembrance Parade at the Cenotaph.

He was ready and waiting when the transport, organised by the British Legion, turned up to collect him. He was loaded aboard in his wheelchair. His colleagues had already been collected, were in their seats and greeted him. There was an air of excitement as they set off to their marshalling point. At nine o'clock, they would form up on Horse Guards Parade in anticipation of the march past. They would join up with all the other detachments as they marched out of the Wellington Barracks at ten o'clock.

Security had been tight this year to reflect the growing threat level in the Capital. The increase had reduced the number of participants, from the ten thousand mark to around eight. Family members had now been reduced, to lessen the risk.

The first Remembrance Service had taken place on the 19th of July 1919 in Whitehall. King George V had established the two minutes silence to be observed on the eleventh hour of the eleventh day of the eleventh month in his Empire address of sixth November of that year. The Cenotaph was built in time for the nineteen twenty Remembrance Parade and Service. The Service was moved in nineteen fifty six to the second Sunday of November, being the nearest Sunday to Armistice Day.

The security checks were robust, but were not focussed on the veterans. If an attack was to materialise, it was anticipated to come from the crowd that would watch the proceedings. Prior to them being accepted to parade, the members of Charlie's association had submitted their details and they had been scrutinised.

There was a genuine fear of an ISIS inspired attack. Threat levels were at an all time high and classified as "exceptional." Snipers were positioned on the roof of the Foreign Office where they could watch the assembled crowd of onlookers. Despite this, all the great and good of the Land would be in attendance.

Proceedings got underway at precisely ten o'clock. Charlie and his Association started their procession some twelve minutes later. It was with a sense of pride that he joined the March Past. The event was televised in its entirety and the whole Nation watched and remembered the bravery of the fallen that maintained the freedom of the living. The veterans were represented by servicemen from around the Globe of all faiths and ethnicities. All had died and made sacrifices. All were honoured annually on this day.

Just before the stroke of eleven a.m. the Queen, Queen Elizabeth II, Britain's longest serving Monarch, walked out to lead the Nation in its contemplation of those that had given their lives for their Country. Dressed in black, she laid the first wreath and stood in silent remembrance for twenty-five minutes. She was followed by the Duke of Edinburgh and the Prince of Wales. The other Royals, the Duke of York, Prince Henry of Wales and the Duke of York laid wreaths and bowed their heads. The Duchess of York, the Duchess of Cornwall and the Countess of Wessex stood reverently on the balcony of the Foreign Office. The Prime Minister, the leader of the opposition, along with the Foreign Secretary and past Prime Ministers all laid wreaths.

At precisely eleven o'clock, the King's Troop, the Royal Horse Artillery, fired the single cannon shot that marked the commencement of the Two Minute Silence. Silence descended across the realm as the dead were remembered.

At two minutes and ten seconds past eleven o'clock, a bomb exploded.

Chapter 37

Earlier, at ten o'clock Sunday morning in Bishops Avenue Hampstead, the Russians, Nikhil, Lesta and Yerik were getting ready to depart. They had received news that the parts for the Learjet had arrived the previous day and that the plane would be ready to fly them back. It was cleared to depart at two o'clock from London City Airport. A van had called earlier to take their suitcases to the airport. They would clear their luggage with Customs when they arrived prior to takeoff.

"I think we should toast our success," said Lesta, producing a bottle of best Russian Vodka at breakfast.

He passed around the shot glasses and together they knocked back the vodka. They were in high spirits. "We are richer and we are once again beloved by the Kremlin thanks to Donald Trump," said Yerik.

Another round was poured. "Donald Trump," was the toast as they drank the next shot.

"One more," said Lesta to "Vladimir Putin," they raised their glasses and drank.

"To Donald Trump and Vladimir Putin long may they be friends," shouted Nikhil.

They all laughed and drank another.

"Gentleman, gentlemen," the valet raised his voice to be heard.

Finally, the three stopped talking and looked his way. "Your car has arrived."

They made their way back to their respective rooms and collected up their remaining bits and pieces that had not been sent ahead to the airport. Ten minutes later, they reassembled back in the vestibule where the staff had congregated to bid farewell.

"Thank you for you service and attention to our requirements," said Yerik, addressing the valet and staff manager. He handed him an envelope." Please distribute this among the staff as a token of our appreciation, now goodbye and thank you all."

They made their way out of the front door to the waiting AJ stretched limousine with the rear doors held open by the uniformed chauffeur. The valet could not resist looking in the envelope. It contained twenty thousand pounds. "Not bad," he thought for a few days work.

They went down the steps. Lesta glanced at his watch. It was a few minutes to eleven. They had plenty of time for the drive to the airport in the Docklands, in East London. He noticed the poppy of the driver's lapel as he handed over his night bag and entered the vehicle, Remembrance Sunday, of course. He wondered if the chauffeur would suddenly freeze in a few minutes and observe the silence.

Nikhil and Yerik handed their bags to the driver and got in the car. The door was closed behind them and the driver placed their overnight bags in the boot, before entering the car and sitting in the driver's seat.

They did not notice as the driver pressed the button of the door panel that applied the child locking system. The doors at the rear and the front passenger door were now locked and could only be opened from the outside, or if the driver released the mechanism. The Russians did not know it, but they were trapped in the car.

The driver opened his door and stepped out of the car. The Russians did not notice at first and carried on their conversation. The driver walked back to the valet and staff gathered on the steps to wave goodbye and show their appreciation.

"Go inside now or you will die."

The valet hesitated. "Now," commanded the driver. Something in the way the man spoke convinced him.

"Inside," he said to the staff. They were used to obeying and did not hesitate. The steps clear, the driver pulled the door closed behind them and then began to run to the side of the mansion, taking his mobile phone from his pocket as he did so.

The Russians became aware that their driver had exited the car and was running away from them. They tried the doors and found them locked. They tried the windows, but they would only come down a few inches to safeguard against the possibility of a child climbing out while the car was in motion.

Panic seized them as the driver disappeared from their view around the edge of the building. Clear, the driver pressed dial on the mobile phone. It took a few seconds to connect. The phone in the boot of the limousine clicked on to receive the driver's call. It triggered the detonator and the bomb in the boot exploded.

The car disintegrated instantly. The bomb had been huge. The biggest ISIS could engineer and fit into a wheel chair. It had been designed to go off at the Cenotaph, killing the Royal family, the politicians and the leaders of the military. ISIS had failed in their attack. It was two minutes and ten seconds past eleven o'clock

Tim reappeared from the side of the building and looked at the burnt out remains of the car. "Rot in hell you bastards." He walked over to the wreckage and placed the three white feathers on the ground next to the incinerated Russians.

Chapter 38

The day before, Saturday morning, Tim called his two bodyguards into the house. "Enough of this protection nonsense Gentleman, today you start doing a proper job as MI5 agents. We are going to stop a terrorist attack."

Ten minutes later, he left the house having contacted the police and The Counter Terrorism response team. He had the back up he required to carry out his plans. He drove off in his car with the two agents following in their car.

While the agents waited outside, he went into the safe house. Nizar had been expecting him. Tim sat across the table and handed him the letter confirming his employment as an agent for MI5. Nizar read the letter and was satisfied. Tim then handed him the envelope.

"Inside is a passport and National Insurance card and fifty thousand pounds. You have your new life."

Nizar checked the contents and put them in his jacket pocket, along with his letter.

"Now you put up or shut up," said Tim and placed the Makarov pistol on the table between them. Nizar picked up the gun. Nizar was familiar with the weapon, having used it many times in Iraq. He checked it was loaded before he put it in his outside pocket.

Nizar got up nodded, they left together and got in Tim's car. Tim signalled for the two agents to follow them. "Where to," Tim asked?

The two cars made their way through the traffic to Jimmy Buari's and Sinita's flat. "You understand what I expect," said Tim?

"I am to accompany Jimmy to the old boys flat and hand over the bomb in the wheelchair. While we are driving back to his flat, you will call in the bomb squad to diffuse the device, rendering it harmless. When we get back you will wait for me to leave and Jimmy will be arrested, with no danger of him doing his suicide bomber martyr bit, as the bomb will no longer be there and it will be harmless even if he tries to trigger it remotely."

"And you walk away with a pocket full of cash and a new identity," said Tim.

Tim dropped Nizar off two blocks from Jimmy's flat. The two agents were parked outside and watched as Jimmy opened the door. The two hugged, as old friends and they both went inside. "He is inside." Tim heard as he answered his phone. He got out of his car and joined the agents in their car watching the flat.

They did not have to wait long. Ten minutes later Jimmy and Nizar walked out of the block carrying the collapsed wheel chair between them. They lifted the hatch on the rear of the old Vauxhall Corsa, loaded it and set of to Charlie Wick's house.

Tim had to admit that the driver had been well trained and tailed the suspects without raising the driver's suspicion. All the pieces were in place for Tim. They watched as the new wheelchair was delivered to the old veteran. Charlie was pleased and could hardly believe the kindness of these two men. It restored his faith in people. Of course, had he known that the wheelchair was loaded with explosive and they were intending to use him as an unwilling suicide bomber, he may well have had a different perspective on human kindness.

Tim and the agents followed Jimmy and Nizar back to Jimmy's flat. "Make sure no one leaves," Tim said, as they got out of the car.

The two agents took up position.

Tim dialled. "Go get them," he said.

Within a matter a minutes, the area was awash with armed police. While Jimmy and Nizar were out delivering a bomb-laden wheelchair, there had been ample time to carry out reconnaissance and plan the detail of the raid. The occupants stood no chance as the security forces entered.

There was the sound of shots. Tim had warned them that there was potentially a bomb on the premises and both terrorist were armed. Jimmy had reached for his phone as the doors and windows crashed in and men rushed them. He planned to dial the device in the wheelchair and at least detonate the bomb. Nizar thinking that Jimmy had realised he had betrayed him was reaching for a gun, drew the Makarov Tim had given him. The swat team having been forewarned by Tim that both terrorists were armed shot first. Both died.

Tim waited as the Counter Terrorist Response Team commander came over to him. "All dead, I retrieved these for you." He handed Tim the money, passport and letter.

Tim walked back to his car, leaving the two MI5 agents in the confusion.

"Mr Wicks, my name is Anthony Burr. I am the head of MI5. May I come in?"

Tim left twenty minutes later and placed the wheelchair with the bomb in the boot of his car. Mr Wicks, an ex military man understood the need for secrecy and Tim was sure that he would never mention their dealings. The bomb was to be detonated by a phone. It was a simple arrangement. Tim checked the phone and retrieved its number. All he had to do was dial it and the bomb would explode.

He had to spend a considerable time sourcing a wheelchair for the veteran invalid so he could get to the Remembrance Parade the following day. He eventually found one and had it delivered later that day.

He then drove to Kenwood House. He thought it fitting, as it was where he and Jackie had held their wedding reception. He waited in the car park and the AJ limousine was delivered. The driver parked the limousine and placed the keys on the top of the rear, driver's side, wheel. Having left the car, the driver was picked up by a colleague that had followed him. They would drive back, together, to their showroom in Central London. Tim collected the key, ensuring that he had not been seen.

****

Ten o'clock Sunday morning. Tim left the house wearing the Chauffeurs uniform and getting in his car and drove to the Kenwood House car park. Luckily, the limousine had not been stolen overnight. His only link to the car would be the call, that he had made from Thames House, to call off the MI5 agents that were to have driven the car. The security call log at Thames House would show the call had been made and his link to AJ Cars would be traceable. It was unavoidable. Tim did not really care. He wanted revenge and he would have it.

He unlocked the boot of the limousine and transferred the wheelchair into it from his car. He then drove the limousine the short distance to the mansion, where the Russians were, at that precise moment, toasting their success.

He waited in the car for the three bastards that had killed his wife to leave. He would have loved to have killed them with his bare hands, but he restrained himself as he held the door open for them to settle into the car. It was a squeeze to get the overnight bags in the boot with the wheelchair already in situ. He squashed the bags in. They were never to be used again, so their condition did not matter.

He walked back to the car park as the police and ambulance rushed to the scene and he drove off. He opened the door to the home that he had shared, so briefly, with his wife and sat looking at her photo on the sideboard. A tear rolled down his check. He sat alone as the light faded into night.

TANKER

Nicholas E Watkins

Also by Nicholas E Watkins

Bank

Dealer

Oligarch

Steel

Hack

About the Author

Nicholas Watkins lives on the Coast with his wife and has four children He is a retired Accountant and has a Degree in Economics. He worked in the City of London for many years.

Nicholas E Watkins

Chapter 1

The Hilux pulled up outside the laboratory and parked. The Moon sat low on the horizon and the first red glow of dawn lit up the dry desert sky. All was still, save for the barking of a dog. Security for this sector of the storage facility was in the hands of the Iraqis. Despite being the only thing moving at that time of the morning, the vehicle had not been challenged and no alarms were sounded as it drove into the inner compound.

On paper, the security around the complex of buildings forming the oil storage facility near Basra was impressive. ISIS had looked at it on many occasions as a potential target, but determined that the security presence was too high and their losses would be unacceptable. The laboratory, situated in its own area away from the main buildings, was, in contrast, perceived as far less of a target by the owners. They had neglected it in their assessment of threat levels, so security here was far less comprehensive.

The occupants of the truck sat waiting tensely in the darkness. They were armed with assault rifles, they would have no hesitation in using them if the need arose. They were committed to the aims of ISIS and would happily die as Martyrs in achieving them.

One of the truck's occupants was no more than a boy of sixteen, but he had the hatred of a thousand years in his heart. His Father and Uncles had all opposed the British occupation. It was part of his being, ingrained from childhood. He had seen how the invaders had gradually been defeated, driven back into their compound and finally isolated into a small, defensive position at the airport. He had helped fire the mortars into their base. He had seen their defeat and knew they were weak. He believed, in the end, ISIS would prevail and the Caliphate would be restored.

His companion was slighter in build but older, in his mid-thirties and with a pock marked face. He had been part of Saddam Hussein's army when the invasion had taken place. When the Coalition forces had overthrown the Dictator, they had disbanded the army. It had left him with a gun and no income. He had no love for Hussein and the then ruling Ba'th party but, he at least had an income and had been able to feed his family. It had not taken long for him to become disillusioned with the so called liberators of his Country and he now saw them as an occupying force.

"He should be here by now," said the older of the two. He looked at his watch. They had been there for nearly an hour. They waited another twenty minutes before the door to the laboratory opened and light spilled out across the compound. They jumped from the cab and, slinging their rifles over their shoulders, ran to the beckoning figure.

"Quiet, follow me," said the man in the lab coat. The technician moved swiftly down the corridors, turning left and right. He used his security pass to open doors and led them further into the building. He stopped and pointed to the radioactive symbol and the warning sign above the door. "My pass will take us no further," he said, leaving them outside the door and returning to his job in another part of the building.

The young boy sneaked a look through the glass panel at the top of the door. "Be careful and keep your head down. What did you see?" said his companion.

"Five of them, they are putting their coats on and getting ready to go home." They knew their shift was due to finish at six a.m. the intruders' information was proving to be correct. Unsupervised, they had developed the habit of knocking off early. They waited quietly until the door opened and the workers began to gather up their belongings. The first worker stepped through the door, bidding goodbye to his colleagues. The boy leapt to his feet and struck him in the face with the butt of his rifle, smashing teeth and

175

breaking bone. The technician staggered backwards into his departing colleagues, his hands clutching his bleeding face. The older of the two pointed his rifle at the group, moving it from side to side. They stepped back, dropping their coats and bags to the floor.

"Put your fucking hands down. This isn't a cowboy movie," he said. "You know what we want, so let's not make this difficult for any of us, OK?"

The workers looked at each other, their team leader, an American, decided to speak, "How do you intend to transport it?"

"Just stick it in a box or bag."

"You will be exposed to a massive dose of radiation. More than an hour or two and you will get very ill and possibly die. Do you realise that? This material needs to be handled with extreme caution."

"Do we look like the kind of people who give a fuck? Now stop pissing about and bag it up for us, unless you'd like to die before it kills us." The head technician began the process of removing the radioactive rods from the calibrating machines and placing them in boxes. He and another technician then unlocked the radiation proof safe and removed the rest of the material, stored for intended future use and put it in the bag along with the rods.

"Give us your cell phones." The workers did as they were told, while the duo ripped the internal phones from the walls. "Now, we are trying to let you live, but we need to escape without you causing us a problem. We'll lock you in and smash the key pad on the other side. We know that will only keep you in here for a very short while, but think on this. If you raise the alarm, all of you will be dead by this time tomorrow and all your families will be dead by the time you get home. You are all Iraqis, apart from this man and you live here. We know you. We know your families. We know where you live and we will kill anyone who betrays us." He drew a small pistol and shot the American head of department in the face to underline the message. The rest of the group cowered and watched in shock as their boss fell to the floor. They had the message loud and clear.

The two men walked out to the truck, struggling under the weight of their radioactive load. "Why are you letting them live? They could raise the alarm?" said the boy.

"The tall ugly one is my cousin."

****

At the petrol station at Qa'im, just inside Iraq on the Syrian border, two ISIS fighters waited in a Ford Galaxy mini bus that was rapidly becoming hot and sticky inside. They had been there for some time, one of them got out and relieved himself. He returned to the bus, "Do you think they are coming? They are very late."

"We wait."

"We are very exposed here. The Security Forces could easily pick us up."

"We wait," said the other with finality.

So they waited and finally the convoy of heavy trucks came through the checkpoint at the border. They were escorted by guards travelling in lightly armoured vehicles. Scant attention was paid to the convoy and they were, more or less, just waved past by the Iraqis. The border was like a sieve and smugglers for the Government and the opposing factions traveled virtually unhindered between Iraq, Turkey and Syria. Trade between the three was probably more vigorous than before the conflict had started. The region had descended into total chaos. Fighters were going one way and insurgents the other, guns in, guns out, drugs and Jihadi brides were passing for good measure. The whole area was a complete security shambles.

The convoy pulled over to swap the escort for the next leg of the journey. The drivers got out of the assorted trucks and HGV's, relieved themselves, ate, faced towards Mecca and prayed. The occupants of the Galaxy joined them in prayers. By now a small fleet of trucks and cars had arrived in the area. It was apparent, that on crossing the border, the truck drivers all had small business ventures going with various locals smuggling items from one side of the border to the other. The gas station had descended into a mini bazaar.

It was a very simple matter for the mini bus occupants to help the driver of the truck carry the large box and place it in the rear of the Galaxy. "Sorry for the delay lads," said the driver "got held up on the road. It seems there was a change in the group that controlled a stretch of the highway. It took an age to sort out the bribe to allow us to pass. It cost me another eight hundred dollars to deliver your goods."

They knew that he was bumping the price up and they guessed he had probably paid a tenth of that. They were in no mood to haggle and gave him the extra. The driver was almost embarrassed by their lack of bargaining, but he, of course, accepted the extra cash.

The Ford Galaxy pulled away from the stop and headed south. If anyone had pointed a Geiger counter at it, they would have seen the needle go off the scale.

******

There were three bombings in Baghdad that day and over a hundred people were either dead or injured. The hospitals were struggling to cope with the injured and dying. ISIS was under pressure and they had been losing ground recently. They were stepping up their bombing campaign, part in retaliation, but also in order to let the World know they were still a force to be reckoned with.

The University was in a state of chaos. A targeted bomb had left the Campus in disarray. Students and staff were among the dead, dying and injured. Ambulances, security forces, police and militia were all engaged in the action. Chaos and panic had spread across the Campus.

The three ISIS members were looking for the Metallurgy Faculty and referring to a map of the building. Soon, they located the secure facility. Security today, however, was totally lacking following the carnage outside. The combination of suicide bombings and the random shooting into the crowd of students had made anyone, with the slightest instinct of self–preservation, get well clear of the Campus. They marched along the corridor to the store of radioactive material and literally, just blew the doors off with a small, plastic explosive charge. They walked back out with a holdall stuffed with the deadly radioactive material, got in a car and drove off. ISIS had just gone nuclear.

Chapter 2

The rain dripped through the hole in the sun awning into the bucket placed on the terrace by the bar owner. There was a large puddle where the bucket had over spilled. A young couple made a dash for the café, the male, wearing flips flops, slipped and nearly fell. The female was more sure footed and reached their table in a less dramatic fashion.

The tables and chairs on the terrace outside the Terminus Café, were a random collection of plastic, cane and metal. They had obviously been collected and replaced over the years and were a total mismatch. The Patron came out and, nearly slipping and falling himself, emptied the bucket that was filling at such a rapid rate in the downpour, served little purpose. Tim looked at the sagging awning, the red stripes faded into the greying white background and wondered, given that the rip in the awning was no bigger than six or seven centimetres, why the owner had not applied a piece of duct tape. Perhaps duct tape was rare in France, or perhaps the owners just could not be bothered and accepted the heyday of the Terminus Café, located directly opposite Menton railway station, had long since passed.

Tim sat with his back to the Café with the open glass door to his right giving him a clear view of the terrace, the station car park and the coming and goings of those entering and leaving the railway station entrance. He stirred his double espresso, three sugars, too many. He kept meaning to cut down, but somehow, forgot each time he put spoon to cup.

To his left there sat the cowboys. Two almost identically dressed men with white beards, stained orange with nicotine. They wore black leather sleeveless jerkins, white stained T shirts and black faded leather cowboy hats with large cross stitching on the brims and crowns. Their sleeping bags and Worldly possessions were stacked under cover in a shop doorway to the left of the Café. Their hands shook as they lifted their coffee to their lips, which the patron's wife had placed on the table in front of them a moment before. They were obviously regulars. The dog that emerged from the Café ran to greet them and was instantly scooped up onto one of their laps by trembling hands.

On Tim's right was a large red and white bag on a chair. Beside it, on the table, were three further, smaller plastic carrier bags stuffed with old clothes. The owner appeared from the Café and stood by the bags. She was in her fifties, hair long and dirty. Her hands also trembled as she struggled to raise a cup to her lips. The drug and alcohol abuse were etched in her face and thin body. She was dressed in flimsy, floral patterned beach trousers, a leopard blouse and a beige wrap around cardigan. Her feet were dirty, her toenails uncut and her toes forced over and under each other by the large bunions on the side of her, flip flop clad, feet. At some stage she must have had a life and obviously had loved her high heeled shoes. Tim imagined her as a young girl, dressed smartly, with her designer shoes and handbags, going to the Casino in Menton, or dancing in the night clubs. No longer desirable, broken and addicted, all her possessions in bags, she relied on the Terminus Café for her morning ablutions. She hopped nervously around the table, taking alternate sips of coffee and dragging on a roughly rolled cigarette that occasionally stuck to her lips.

Tim took another sip of his very sweet coffee and looked up to see a group of four men running from a black van to the cover of the terrace. There was more slipping and sliding on the treacherous wet tiles before they reached the safety of the chairs and sat at a table. The bucket was now overflowing, as the rain continued to pour down. Thunder could be heard in the distance. The patron appeared with croissants and coffees and greeted the arrivals. Their jackets showed them to be railway workers. A fifth man dashed in and joined them and was greeted loudly by his co-workers.

So far, not one of the Café's customers fitted the bill of the man he was expecting to meet. He ordered another espresso and again put too much sugar in it. Tim, whose real name was Anthony Burr, had acquired the nick-name from his schoolmates. They had been unable to resist the opportunity for the joke, a "chip off the old block, timber," so the name stuck with him. He had been waiting at the Café for nearly an hour so far. Tim was forty one and looked out of place as he sat in the rain in the faded establishment. His clothes were a cut far above those of the other customers and his well-groomed appearance made him conspicuously noticeable. He felt uncomfortable.

This weekend had certainly not turned out as expected. He had anticipated spending a jolly few days at the Hotel Lewes in Monaco, watching the Grand Prix and perhaps getting a bit of sun. Today was race day and he had his place reserved on a nice yacht facing the track. Instead, he was sat, in probably the grubbiest café in the Cote D'Azure, doing someone else's job in the rain.

He had joined the civil service after he left Selwyn, Cambridge. He had done well enough, with a two one degree, to get a job in the Home Office. After a few years he was transferred to help out the long suffering Ambassador in Paris, where he would use his knowledge of foreign affairs to brief him daily with what was happening in the World. Technically, he was employed as an intelligence officer. Sounded like a spy but, in reality, he read the local papers, checked the briefings from the various government departments and made sure the Ambassador had a clear picture of the current situation and a clear understanding of what the current policy thinking was. After working in Thames House for a couple of years, he finally got Paris and was on this beano in Monaco. Along with the Ambassador, staff, some trade delegation chaps, he had managed to wangle the invite for himself to watch the Grand Prix, from a yacht booked by the Turkish trade delegation, in the Marina.

A note had been passed to the Ambassador's aide and as they had no one spare, here he was sat in the rain, waiting to meet a contact who, presumably, had a bit of inside information on trade or some such thing, while everyone else was tucking into a champagne breakfast on a luxury yacht.

He looked at his watch. His contact was late. The couple had left and the railway workers were making their way across the car park to the station. The itinerant cowboys appeared to be texting. How odd the World was. Nowhere to sleep, but you had a mobile phone. The table on the other side of the door was now occupied by a black man with a large suitcase on wheels, not his contact, a traveller perhaps? Not so, he clearly was the supply centre for the horde of beach hawkers that sold cheap goods on the beaches. He was approached by further Africans and goods were swapped around and money changed hands. The bag lady was looking at a mobile phone on offer from a beach trader, but there was still no sign of his contact.

The rain had stopped, the hills beyond were still bathed in a grey mist and rain and the distant sound of thunder could still be heard. He looked at his phone, checking the Grand Prix update. It was raining in Mote Carlo as well and the start of the race was under threat. He had now waited for nearly an hour and half. Enough he thought and made his way inside to settle up.

No one was to be seen, clearly service was not a priority at the Terminus Café. He heard voices from a side room. He stood and waited for a while. In the end, with no sign of anyone, he made his way towards the sound. He stood in the doorway. The family were sat around a table, covered with a red and white plastic check table cloth, having their breakfast. He stood. They looked quizzically at

183

him. "The bill," he said.

Reluctantly, the wife got to her feet and making him feel as though he was a nuisance by being a paying customer, she walked to the bar.. He followed her. His French was poor, GCSE standard. He could not understand the number being requested and pointed to the till which should have displayed the amount or printed off a bill but did neither. This caused a blast of French. The till was clearly not in the regular habit of being used. Cash in hand was the order of the day here. He removed ten euros and offered it to her. Success, change and he tipped her fifty cents. He had to admit, that although not salubrious, the Terminus Café was value for money.

He turned to leave, feeling that the morning had been a waste of time and effort. "Monsieur pour vous?" she handed him an envelope from behind the bar. It was addressed "L'homme Angletere," vague but effective.

Outside, he pulled out the note and read." Hotel Belgique, Room 15, Rue de la Gare. After 10, the concierge goes at 9. Code 8476, Stereogram." His heart sank. He would have to come back tonight. This was not the fun break he had hoped for.

He realised he was already in the Rue de la Gare. He glanced down the road and could clearly see the Hotel Belgique. He considered the note. "Who calls them self Stereogram?" he said to himself as he made his way across the car park to the railway station.

The rain had stopped in Menton, at least. He had purchased a return ticket in Monaco, so he went straight to the platform. The train was on time, but crowded with race goers. The journey took ten minutes with two stops. Then the problems began. He knew he needed to buy his ticket now for his trip back to Menton that evening. The queues would be huge after the race. Leaving the train, he tried to make his way to the main ticket concourse, but was blocked by a group of race officials. The crowds were being controlled by the seat numbers to their positions around the circuit. He tried to explain that he wished only to purchase a ticket, but that was clearly not in the remit of the marshals who ushered him off in the opposite direction. The station, he had to admit, was spectacular, clad in pink marble and spotlessly clean. Despite its architecture and splendour, he was losing interest in its elegance as he walked the whole underground route to end up at the other end of the town.

The streets were packed with race goers, street traders and race officials marshaling the pedestrians. Everywhere was jammed and everyone, it appeared, was going in the opposite direction to him. The rain had started again and was tipping down. He was very wet and fed up by the time he finally made it back to the station ticket office. He finally bought his return ticket to Menton. It was nearly two o'clock by the time he returned to the hotel to find everyone had left for the yacht. A pass to allow him access to the Marina had been left behind the desk, but he would have to get himself there. The Ambassador and the rest of the party had a nice escorted limo drive. He, on the other hand, would be back in the crowd, marshalled and wet. He set off with his recent purchase of a grey and white souvenir Monaco umbrella.

Chapter 3

Berat woke to the smell of tea, simit bread and the sound of hammering downstairs. His Mother was busy in the room next door, where she and his Father slept and where they all ate and watched television. Although it was just seven in the morning, he knew his Father had been up for hours working in the shop downstairs.

The whole flat smelt of leather, always of leather. They lived above his Father's cobblers shop. By the time he and his brothers were fed in the morning and went down the stairs to go to school, his Father would be busy at work. Piles of shoes were stacked up in the house, in the shop or outside waiting in pairs on the pavement, either for sale or collection. His Father was not the only cobbler in the street. The whole street up and down had the scene repeated. His trip anywhere, always started by passing between piles of footwear on the pavement surrounding his home in either direction.

His friends Emir and Ahmet were waiting to walk to school with him, He made his way past shoes and said goodbye to his Father who sat on the floor with a bradawl in his hand and a shoe on the last. His Father always said, "Work hard and get an education. You don't want to end up doing this all your life."

He took on board what his Father had said. So he had worked hard and had an education. Now a grown man, he sat on the wall overlooking the Bosphorus. The noise of the traffic on the road behind him was deafening. Vehicles of all shapes, sizes and ages

186

streamed past, many blasting thick plumes of oil burning smoke. He suspected that Turkish emissions laws for vehicles, like many other laws, were not strictly enforced. In some ways the Country had come a long way since he was a child, in others it was going backwards. Ataturk, the Father of the modern Country, had created a secular government distinct from the religion. For a while, with the exception of the odd military coup, it had functioned, but now the State was more repressive and fundamentalism was on the rise.

Stretching in front of him was the sea, glistening with patches of oil and pollution. The oil tankers lined up to enter the Bosphorus, the twenty mile long north-south strait that joins the Sea of Marmara to the Black Sea and separates Europe and Asia. The ships were so large and appeared so close that you felt you could reach out and touch them. They seemed like toy boats in a bath. He had grown up with this sight all his life, but it still continued to captivate him. Now, in his mid-thirties, working as a civil servant, he longed for the simplicity in his life as it had been as a child, playing in the streets of Istanbul.

The Bosporus was just a part of his everyday life, from childhood he had taken it for granted. He remembered, as he gazed on the comings and goings of the vast ships, the day he had gone to University. His Father had gathered the whole family, brothers, cousins, aunts, uncles and friends to celebrate. His Father's pride was so great that he felt the burden to succeed weighing on him. He set himself to nothing but study and achievement. He did succeed, a first class degree followed by a masters and a well-paid secure job in government. He had taken extra language courses and spoke perfect French and English. He now travelled frequently around the World, acting as translator for the great and good in government and commerce. He knew that the English name Bosphorus came from the Greek bous, meaning cow and poros, meaning crossing, cow crossing. The legend went that Zeus had an affair with Io. When his wife Hera got wind of it she turned Io in a cow and created a horsefly to sting her bottom. It hurt so much that Io, the now cow, jumped across the strait.

He smiled to himself as he thought of cows jumping over the queue of tankers waiting to move oil around the Globe. His smile faded as he thought of Emir and Ahmet, brothers. He had grown up with them, shared school, fights, and sexual adventures. They were more like his own brothers or his family than friends. Their lives, of course, had diverged, he to University while they had remained in the grubby backstreets of Istanbul scraping a living as best they could. They were still close, but their life experiences were separated by a gulf wider than the Bosporus. He knew that, with their increasing frustrations and poverty, they had become more and more fundamentalist in their beliefs.

Behind him he could hear the call to prayers ringing out across the city. It was not that he was a bad Muslim, it was that he was more tolerant and inclined to live and let live. He valued peace. He had seen enough suffering acting as a translator around the Globe to know that the World did not need a helping hand down the road to more pain. Ahmet, the younger of the two brothers, had first become involved actively with the Fundamentalist Brotherhood when he was in his late teens. Like all young men, he had imagined himself the hero, fighting for truth and Allah, saving the poor, fighting the good fight. Berat reflected, as a child watching the old kids' television programs of jousting knights rescuing damsels, he had also seen its appeal. He knew all young boys yearned to be heroes and brave and the Muslim Brotherhood movement offered the chance to fight the corrupt and gain glory.

Ahmet started attending the more hard-core seminars held at the Mosques, meeting with other frustrated young men and searching the internet for like-minded individuals. It was not long before his brother Emir was being drawn into the more radical form of Islam as well. Now in their thirties, they wanted change. The idea of secular government was an insult to them, their beliefs and above all, to Allah. A trip to Syria had hardened their resolve and they were committed to the cause. Berat, to an extent, humoured them, not wishing to lose touch with that part of his life and his roots in the streets of Istanbul. He had been guilty, to an extent, of letting them think he was right there with them.

Celik, his wife was their younger sister. Berat had known her as the little pest that the three of them had teased as children. That had changed one summer when he came back from University. They fell in love and married. She was a good wife but shared many of her brothers' beliefs. Berat knew that, as her husband, she respected his wishes and never voiced her opinions to his more secular colleagues they mixed with.

As he sat watching the sun coming down and turning the sky bright red, yellow and lavender, it seemed to him that it was like an omen. His World was changing, he had not asked for it but it was. He now had choices, choices that Allah should ask no man to make.

Berat had been excited at being part of the delegation going to Monte Carlo. Of course, French was his specialist language and he would head the team of four translators working with him. It was a chance to influence the British. They all knew their support was key to Turkey's entry into the European Union. He knew that every opportunity would be taken to polish their record on human rights, their commitment to fighting terrorism and to demonstrate their commitment to the West.

He was finalising the details with his team when Yosuf had asked him to step into his office. Berat immediately sensed that this was not the usual, checking on final details, type of meeting.

"Take a seat," Yosuf commanded. This was unusual, Yosuf was not a command type of person. Berat feared he had made an error and was to be hauled over the coals. "There is a problem, a big problem," Berat feared that his job was on the line as Yosuf continued.

189

"You are married to Celik and she has two brothers, does she not, Emir and Ahmet?" he did not pause for a reply." "As I said, there is a problem." He seemed to struggle to find the words to continue. The word problem hung in the air. He took a deep breath. "They are to be arrested."

Berat's mouth hung open in surprise, "Arrested, for what."

"Security matters"

"My wife?"

"She will be fine, do not worry on that account; I have vouched for you both. I told them I know you to be a loyal servant of the State and totally dependable."

At that moment Berat realised his suspicions of Yosuf were well founded. He had always suspected that there was far more to Yosuf's role than just head of the Foreign Office translation department. He now realised, in that role, Yosuf could travel around and liaise with his Country's espionage resources globally. He had worked with him for nearly seven years and this confirmed that he was definitely part of Counter Intelligence. With hindsight, Berat began to see historic events in a new light, burglaries, disappearances and killings fell into focus. He was not just a translator. He was part of the cover for the State to carry out what it needed to do.

"You realise you must not warn them, nor tell your wife, don't you?"

Berat nodded, but he knew that he would and that decision would change his life for ever.

Yosuf knew he should not have warned Berat, but he was fundamentally a decent man. Turkey was such a contradiction. The State was becoming more oppressive, reversing women's rights and curtailing the media, on the other hand it was fighting a campaign against ISIS and terrorism. He knew Berat was a good man and he genuinely hoped that with this warning, he would keep himself and his wife well clear of her radical brothers. His hopes were to be in vain.

Berat knew he would betray his boss, even as he was warned to stay silent, but he also knew he could not stand by and not warn his wife. He left the office and changing trams had made his way to the Grand Bazaar. He knew this could be a trap to test his loyalty and feared that he may be followed. He hoped that the most crowded area in Istanbul would give him a chance of not being observed by anyone sent to follow him. He mingled in the crowds, stopped, doubled back and hoped he had avoided a tail if there had been one. He entered the phone shop.

Berat had purchased the cell phone for cash with credit on it. Sent the text to Celik warning her, with instructions for her to destroy her phone and dispose of the sim card. All the authorities could trace then would be an anonymous text from an unregistered phone, but the content of the message could not be retrieved. Berat removed the sim from his new phone, pulled out the battery and dumped it.

Celik ran down the road looking from side to side. She knew people were watching her. She was sweating and panicking. She ran as fast as she could. The text had been clear "Your brothers are to be arrested for terrorism. Do not use any phones, they are tapped, warn them and destroy evidence."

Her lungs hurt as she ran up the winding staircase to the flat where her brothers were. She banged on the door. The door opened onto a normal scene. "Grand Theft Auto" was paused on the PlayStation, they had been drinking coke and eating crisps as they played.

"What's all this noise," asked Ahmet, standing in the doorway dressed in shorts. "Is there a fire?" She pushed past into the room.

191

"The police are coming and you must get rid of any incriminating evidence, do not use the phones." The look of panic was in their eyes. Frantic activity began as she left.

"Take this. Someone will contact you for it," Emir pushed a memory stick into her hand. She kissed her brothers and ran again. She was a street away when she heard the sirens.

When Berat arrived home he found Celik upset and distraught. She had followed his instruction to the letter. "They were arrested. I warned them and they gave me this." she gave him the memory stick. Berat plugged it into his computer, but could make no sense of its contents. He did know, however, what was on it should be in the hands of the State, but handing it over would put the final nail in the coffin of his own wife and her family. He could destroy it and not warn anyone, but he was sure that that would result in the deaths of innocents in their hundreds or more. The alternative of giving it to ISIS, when they contacted Celik, which they surely would, was also not an option.

Chapter 4

The race was due to start at four and it rained like it can only rain on the Mediterranean Coast. Warm and wet, it continued to rain and then, as if on cue, the rain eased and the race started under the safety car. It did not take long before the drivers became bored with driving in convoy so they decided that the conditions were good enough and the air was filled with the full glorious roar of Mercedes, McLaren, Renault and Ferrari. It was loud, Formula 1 loud. The cars were a blur as they passed in front of the yacht. The Lady Heloise, moored in Monaco, was a hundred million dollars' worth of some one's toy that looked like it had never set to sea in its life.

She was moored at a beautiful location on the straight with bends visible at both ends. The Marshals in their red overalls lined the track along the quayside in front of them. The lower deck had been laid out as a dance and buffet area, while the upper decks were for the Brits and drinkers whose glasses were constantly filled with champagne. The lower deck was crowded with beautiful people. A video operator filmed the guests from every angle with a camera suspended from a gimbal and a stills photographer snapped incessantly. A black girl, with almost an afro, in a very flimsy bright yellow dress and her white friend in a bikini made sure they danced their way into every shot. Other young girls were scattered around like cushions to add to the décor.

Tim positioned himself on the top deck and watched the cars going round the track behind the safety car, He then watched as Verstappen crashed and his Red Bull car was hoisted clear off the

193

track by a crane, as the race continued under the virtual safety car. The virtual safety car required the cars not to overtake and follow the car in front at a non-race pace until the green flag sign was illuminated, signaling full racing was to recommence. As the race resumed, Tim was approached by the Ambassador.

"Ah you made it? Sorry we couldn't hang on for you, but as you know there is the schedule to keep to in all these affairs." He smiled broadly as he spoke. He had a full face, a face that seemed to ooze affability and understanding and eyes that focussed on whomever he was speaking to, letting you know that you had his full, undivided attention. It made no difference if you were the cleaner or the Premier of China, that face was always totally absorbed and interested in what you had to say. He did actually sound genuinely sorry for leaving Tim to wander through the crowds in the pouring rain while he was chauffeured in luxury.

"No problem. I enjoyed the walk and needed the exercise," Tim lied.

Jason Delonge was your typical old Etonian, totally confident, comfortable in every situation and knew anybody who was worth knowing, added to that, he had obtained the trendy must have Philosophy, Politics and Economics first from Oxford, suits from Dege and Skinner in Saville Row and was set for all steam ahead in the diplomatic World of today.

Tim knew that Jason was actually brilliant at his job, but couldn't help feeling a bit irritated by how easy it had come to him. Tim also had his suits made by Nick at Dege and Skinner, but he always felt like he did not quite belong there and somehow the suits seemed to look better on the Ambassador. In truth the Ambassador had run to a paunch while Tim worked out in the gym daily and had practised martial arts since joining the society at Cambridge.

The conversation could only take part in short bursts in the brief relative quiet when the cars were not flying past. "How did your trip to Menton go?

"Nobody turned up," he picked the wrong moment to reply. Clearly the Ambassador had not heard a word, but by force of habit, seemed fully engaged.

"That's good then. You can sort it out on Monday with the naughty boys." He wandered off heading towards the decorations dancing on the lower deck. Tim turned his attention back to the Grand Prix. The naughty boys referenced were the attachés assigned by MI6. The spies every embassy had.

"Hi." He turned to see an oriental girl in her mid-twenties with a massive straw hat garnished with flowers, wearing what appeared to be a recreation of a Mary Quant lace mini dress. His eyes were automatically drawn to her chest where her nipples were clearly visible through the gaps in the crocheted work. She was stunning, too young, too obviously on the make but very pleasing to look at.

"Hello, are you enjoying the race?" he asked.

The roar of the engines did not make conversation easy. He did establish that she was planning to be an actress, model or something in PR and that she knew a great deal about shoes and fashion. Clearly they had a great deal in common. He liked the look of her body and she liked his career prospects and the fact he was divorced with no children.

He had met his wife at University and they moved in together for the second year in a house share. The third year at Selwyn meant he had a room in the College, so there had been a brief separation before they reunited in and moved to London. In hindsight, he probably would have done worse on his course if he had lived with her in the third year. She obtained her first without breaking sweat. She had the brains. They married when they got to thirty and planned on children.

Then it all started to go wrong. Lisa's career went cosmic. A whole new world, she was a banker, then a fund manager. He saw the change in her. There was nothing he could do. He knew he was boring, pedestrian, and irrelevant. She was dynamic, energised and a winner. They were no longer the people they were at Cambridge. They were now poles apart. The divorce had been quick, more painless for him than for her. But life goes on.

He looked at the girl standing beside him and decided that life was not going to go on with her that day. He made his excuses and watched as Roseberg lost pole allowing Hamilton to go on to win.

In the office on the lower deck, the translators, provided by the Turks, were lacking in co-ordination and leadership. Yosuf was furious. "Where the fuck is Berat?" He shouted at his aide.

Chapter 5

Booking the Hotel Belgique had taken Berat a few clicks the night before and there had been no queue at Mote Carlo for his return ticket to Menton. It was early Sunday morning and most of his colleagues would just be making their way down for breakfast. He made his way along the long marbled halls to platform two. The platform was virtually empty. He immediately spotted the Englishman from the British group waiting for the same train. He recognised him from the cocktail party on the Friday night and the qualifying session which they all watched from the Lady Heloise. They had not spoken, but he was pretty certain he would recognise him in turn.

He had not expected this turn of events. He, in no way wanted to be identified as the source of the information. Turkey was a member of NATO and shared intelligence with the other member States. One slip and his name would be out and the Turkish authorities would know that he had aided his brothers in-law.

He sat down on the benches that were positioned at intervals along the platform. Unlike most seating on station platforms, they did not face the rail track but were positioned at right angles facing the bench opposite. There was a middle aged man and a teenage girl sitting opposite him. They were very engrossed in each other. Berat now had his back to Tim.

Berat's mind raced. He needed to rid himself of the memory stick, memory sticks to be accurate. He had taken the precaution of copying the original. He could feel them like two enormous weights

197

in his jacket pocket. In hindsight, his plan of meeting a British agent in a hotel room seemed a bit simplistic. Pass an anonymous note, meet a spy, dump the information and go home to a normal life. Now it seemed far more complicated. True, he wanted to prevent the deaths of innocent people at the hands of ISIS, but he did not want the source of the information traced back to him and his wife,

He jumped as a train rushed through the station without stopping, shaking him from his thoughts. His stomach churned with nerves and he felt himself sweating, despite the cool of the subterranean platform. He took several deep breaths in an attempt to calm himself. He needed to come up with an alternative plan that did not reveal him as the source and expose his links to his brothers in-law.

The Menton train pulled in on time. He remained seated and watched as Tim boarded the train. At the last instant he jumped up and also boarded. The journey was only around ten minutes with just two stops. As the train pulled into Menton station, he made sure to be by the doors. Pressing the button to open the doors, he hurried from the train and platform. On exiting the station he instantly saw the Café across the car park. From his visit to Google, he knew that the hotel Belgique was just a hundred metres past the Café on the road to its left.

There were a few diners in the dining room having breakfast, but no-one else to be seen in the Hotel Belgique. He had entered via a glass door into an outer lobby and then into what was the reception area. There was a desk with an open door to the right which led to the dining room. He looked on the reception counter for a bell or something. There were the usual brochures for things to do in the area and a note saying the desk was manned from seven to eleven in the morning and five till nine in the evening. In the dining a room a short black woman appeared carrying breakfasts and placed them on a diner's table.

She saw him "Just a moment," she called as she went behind the bar at the end of the dining room and began to operate the espresso machine. Coffee served she came to the desk. "You were due yesterday evening, two nights," she said.

"Delayed," he had booked for two nights so he would have the room available today. She gave him the key to room fifteen and the code to the front door, should he need to get in after nine in the evening. He paid in cash.

To the left of the desk was a grubby grey, marble spiral staircase. Room fifteen was on the second floor. The grout between the marble tiles on the steps was black and the handrail wobbled as he grabbed it walking upwards. The hotel had its location on its side, directly by the rail Station but very little else. It had been neglected for years. Probably the only time it even approached being full was during the Grand Prix. This was borne out by the diners, who either wore their supported teams logos and colours on their clothing or on their caps. He climbed the stairs to the first floor, paused on the landing and continued up to the top floor of the building.

Room fifteen had a double bed to the left as you entered and a single along the wall at the bottom. A small table, an old chair and a hang rail completed the furnishings. To the right there was a stud wall that didn't reach the ceiling. This contained the smallest basin, toilet and shower known to man. He sat on the chair and considered the turn of events. He placed the two memory sticks on the table. He felt relief at relinquishing them, even if he had only distanced himself from them by a few inches.

Oligarch

Also by Nicholas E Watkins

Tanker

Dealer

Bank

Steel

Hack

Printed in Great Britain
by Amazon